NOT THE SHADOW OF A MAN

Dorothy Davies

NOT THE SHADOW OF A MAN

Fiction4All

Fiction4All
www.fiction4all.com

This Edition
Published 2017

Dedication

Dedicated to the memory of Jacquetta Wydeville
17th January 1416 – 30th May 1472

And to the memory of every woman who was persecuted or executed for being a 'witch'. Jacquetta was acquitted of the charges, but she remembers to this day those who were not. 'Wise women' who were – and are – mediums, were – and are – misunderstood, then and now. Jacquetta is aware this is something I know well.

(Found on a motto calendar.)
It is surprising how few people are willing to support the truth, and how many people are willing to accept the deceit

From Immortality
Olton Pools, Sidgwick and Jackson Ltd.,1917

There in the midst of all these words shall be
Our names, our ghosts, our immortality.

6

Jacquetta's dedication:

This book is dedicated, with the greatest love imaginable, to my husband Richard Wydeville, the man who made my life worthwhile. His love saw me through all the bad times. His execution was the most dreadful thing that ever happened to me.

I must at this time remember my children: Elizabeth who became Queen of England, Antony, who became a shining star in the court of Edward IV and all the other siblings who made good marriages and left their mark on life. Through them the Wydeville name lives on, whichever way you choose to spell it.

I wish to acknowledge with love this channel who has worked hard for the Wydevilles and is continuing to work for the Wydevilles. No one else has shown this level of dedication to us. Dear one, I thank you.

Union
From Seeds of time by John Drinkwater, Sidgwick & Jackson Ltd., 1921

I
Suppose me dead; think of the man you made,
A moment, but as earth unbreathing more,
His garments folded, and his reckoning paid
Of love, and faith, and fame; then, as before
A chronicle all done, with *finis* writ,
Ask if the man you made had truly been
More worth your pride and daily watching wit
Had fear of you one passage cancelled clean.

Would you not say, serenely gospelled then,
"I taught him faith, I bade his word be said
Fearing no challenge nor reproof of men;

And had the happy courage that I bred
Once brought me chill obedience for wage,
This chronicle had been a poorer page."

II
For, dear, I can but serve you at the rate
That is my heart's occasion, that is all;
If I deny myself and with you wait,
It is not I, however you may call;
Something of me must go, if I deny,
Though in denial shall be with you still
A body walking and a watchful eye.
The patient service of an impoverished will.

For if the love that loved, and chose, and came
Ever again to you, nor ever found
Estrangement in far absences, nor blame
For pilgrimage to other Edens bound.
Should know one beauty by your will denied,
Thenceforth how should old faith be satisfied?

III
But when you bid me go as beauty calls,
Knowing that my desire could follow none
But fair vocation, and that intervals
In honest love are still love's errands done,
When you upon my embarkation wait,
And cry O Keel! forth in pursuit of spring,
All Archipelagos to navigate.
You are my ship, and this your voyaging" –

Then nothing lets between your sovran pride
And all my kingdom, nor is poor pretence
That over all my fortunes you preside
When half my levies are rebellious pence;
Then do you govern that your craft began,
A man, and not the shadow of a man.

Chapter One

Am I not royal? Am I not descended from royalty? Was I not a worthy person to be in court in London, the centre of the world? Of course I was.

Why then did they look at me as if I should not be there, as if a 'mere' duchess should not be capable of walking the same flagstone floors as they, as if her shoes were not of the finest silk and the most delicate of beadwork and her clothes were not the very latest in fashion design and materials? I assure you they did look at me thus and I also assure you that my clothes were the very latest, so they had no reason to do that.

Not everyone took that attitude, I hasten to add. Not everyone looked at me in such a way. Only those who were of what they considered – wrongly - to be higher rank or breeding than myself. Maybe I should have declared my background a little more, spoken of the court of Luxemburg, the splendid buildings which put these shabby London ones to shame by their very glory, speak of the tapestries, the art, the music, the learning, the –

But would they not have considered that I boasted? After all, none had set foot there and had no way of knowing if what I said was true or untrue. Knowing their minds, they would say it was untrue, that I lived in a dream world where all is right and I am superior to them in every way.

I am.

They, people who look down their patrician noses at me, think because they are of English nobility, those of us who have come from 'other countries' are not equal to them. So let me tell them, every last one of them, my father was Peter I of Luxembourg, Count of Saint-Pol and hereditary Count of Brienne. That's enough titles to guarantee any man a place at the royal occasions in Europe. My mother was Margaret de Baux, daughter of Francois de Baux, duke of Andria and Sueva Orsini. Do I need to go on? Is it not enough to know that I was - and am - the eighth generation descendant of King John? Trace it back; see that I am actually related to English royalty. I almost want to say 'take that' but it would be childish and despite my desire to stamp my foot and say 'take that, you English upstarts who have little to no history to match mine!' I will not do it. I will retain the dignity I had from the start.

I recall my mother saying, in one of her endless lectures, 'Jacquetta, my dear daughter, no matter what provocation you suffer, be dignified. Do not give them ammunition to throw at you, for they who are newcomers to the ranks of the mighty will seek to bring down those who are entitled to be in the ranks of the mighty.' So it has been throughout my life. I grew up associating with the highest in European aristocracy and never gave it a thought that life would be anything but perfect, always there would be money, food beyond needs, comfort beyond requirements, clothes for every occasion and some which were just there for my pleasure should I decide to wear them.

These changed year by year as I grew taller and fuller, as I went from lisping apparently precocious child - so I am told – to the woman who, in one ceremony, became a duchess.

In truth, if you want the truth, I was above all of them in rank, I was second only to the Queen when she arrived and so they had no right, none at all, to look down on me. I was determined to fight back in the only way I knew, guile and skill. And I did it, didn't I?

Oh I know the Wydevilles were vastly unpopular, the court disliked my schemes, my dynastic dreams which all came true, but they had no choice and that is the good thing, which I gloated over at the time. They could try and look down on me, but they had no choice but to accept us, did they?

But before then ... I grew up in a magnificent home in Luxembourg. Well, to me it was magnificent, anyway. It was like a small castle, it had turrets and towers, it had battlements and windows, stairs everywhere, what I thought of as a Great Hall with the tallest ceiling in the world, I thought at the time. It was hung with tapestries, arrases if you prefer, with shields and swords and armour and had rushes, great thick layers of them, thrown on the stone floors. Yes, it was in many respects like an English castle, ones I was used to seeing later in my life, but – there was an elegance about my home that was lacking in the castles I stayed in and visited in England. Or is it my childhood memories which bring this to me now? Were there not ornate carvings on the huge arches that took you from room to corridor to room, were there not niches in which Mother set flowers to lighten the place, for it was, apart from the tapestries, grey stone and grey mortar and it could bring down the spirits if it were not lightened in some way. I recall many flickering torches lit most of the time, for the rooms were dark and the corridors, even with their many windows, also dark because of the heaviness and thickness of the walls. I was surprised when I came to England to find no one had flowers anywhere in their great homes. I was used to that and missed it.

My room was small so consequently it was warm. I had a fine carved bed, table, closet, mirror which I prized, thick rugs and thick coverlets. I had nursemaids and servants who kept a fire burning all winter and the windows open to the air all summer. I loved it. That was my sanctuary when everything got too much for me.

My upbringing was strict. Nurses, nursemaids, tutors, companions, all sought to do one thing, impress upon me my status in life. In my eyes I was a Princess. To the world I was European royalty, with an immaculate pedigree. Ask some of those who look down on us Wydevilles what their pedigree is. I wonder if they will answer you. Forgive me for constantly referring to 'them' and 'those' but my life, from the time I married my first and indeed my second husband, seemed to be one of conflict with those who would try and denigrate my status. Jealousy, I am assured it was just jealousy but that is difficult to live with when you are smiled at to your face and the knives are out if you turn your back.

There were those who insisted only the English aristocracy knew how to educate their children. Wrong again! For me, there were lessons and manners at all times to remember, no matter who was there. I was taught the right way to greet a duke, an earl, a count and so on, how to eat at table, how to converse, to dance, to be in a room or ballroom full of people and not let anyone feel you were neglecting them. I would go to bed at times with my head spinning with do's and don'ts. And if I got something wrong? There was always a strap handy and that stung. I avoided it if at all possible.

The correct way of deferring to those of higher rank to me was inculcated in me from a very early age. I knew if I had children, that had to be passed on to them, too. Nothing was more important than treating those above you with the correct form of respect and addressing them in the right way, too. Anything else would cause offence. These were matters held in very high regard by all aristocratic people.

My parents were distant people; I was relegated to the care of the nurses, nursemaids, tutors and companions. If I saw my parents, it was a formal occasion. I had to be washed, dressed, tutored and subdued before I was allowed into their presence. They seemed like remote figures to me, I was told to love them but what was the meaning of the word 'love' when applied to those who patted my head, told me I was pretty and to be good and then dismiss me? Respect, fear, yes, but not love.

I would tell the doll I treasured, a gift from an aunt who seemed to understand more than my mother about the needs of small girls, that when I grew old enough to have children, I would not be a distant mother. I would be with them, listen to them, play with them, watch their growing up on a daily basis, not a once a week visit. I would care for them in every way, including working to secure their future lives. My doll would stare back at me with knowing eyes. She understood my need to make a determination for the future to counteract the loneliness of the present. And it was lonely. Very much left to my own devices, with kittens to play with and the occasional friend, but within the house, only what seemed to me to be aged nurses, tutors and servants to take care of me.

What I thought of as my growing years, my young adult years, seemed to consist of dances, dinners, formal balls, visits to other families, polite conversation and long dull evenings of not very much. I loved fashion; colour, lace trimmings and materials but few others shared my interests. Gowns, yes, the girls I met could discuss gowns for an eternity but not what they were made of or how to embellish what you already had by changing a collar, altering the cuffs, adding a petticoat and slashing the overskirt and edging it with lace and creating a new look – they would stare at me and then giggle, "Oh Jacquetta, what quaint ideas you have!" Were they quaint? I thought them innovative and interesting but I could not get others to see this. I abandoned that subject immediately. Instead I listened patiently to their talk of suitable suitors, would this one do or that, did he have sufficient background, enough money, enough contacts, not was he a good person, would he make them happy. Somehow 'happiness' was not meant to be part of our lives.

I wondered; I even talked to my nurse about who I would marry. I had been a 'woman' for a year or more, able to bear children, fit for the role of a wife but no one person had been presented to me as a possible husband and companion for the rest of my life. The nurse had no idea why the subject had not been raised with me or indeed any part of the family. She knew nothing and that was a surprise to us both, for she mingled with all the servants and knew all the gossip. It was through this I knew that my mother and father did not share a bed or even a room, that they lived virtually separate lives. I made up my mind then that when I married, I would be a wife in every sense, I would share my husband's life in every way. Just as I had plans to be in my children's lives every day, so I would be wife and companion to whoever my parents dictated I would marry.

Two major decisions. One that I would be wife and companion to my husband, two that I would be a proper mother and be with my children, supervise them, watch over them, guide them and work for them. I never deviated from those decisions, not once in my life.

My friends, one by one, were getting married. I went to this wedding and that, saw the smiling faces of some and the look of desperation in the eyes of others, especially the younger ones, for the men they were to be married to were old, infirm, ugly, unbecoming. Some even looked cruel, to me anyway. I saw the apprehension on their faces and wondered afresh at the endless chatter I had endured about who they would marry, what contacts they had to make them a worthwhile partner. It seemed it was all very well to talk of these things but when the moment came to be tied to that person forever, the situation was rather different. When you faced a lifetime of living with someone you might come to hate…

In that moment I realised my mother was not in love with my father and so they had separate rooms and separate lives. I didn't want that. I wanted to be in love. I wanted the closeness of the emotion called love, if I could find out what it was. My friends talked of it endlessly, saying they 'loved' this one or that, but it seemed to me their feelings were transient, for it would change after a few months and some other handsome man would be the love of the moment.

This went on for some time, until one day my mother called me to her room and told me, abruptly, a marriage had been arranged. I was to marry John of Lancaster. When I asked who he was, she told me, with a pursing of her lips as if annoyed that I did not know, that he was the 1st duke of Bedford. I asked what background he had, recalling the many conversations I had endured with the other girls of my age.

So she told me. I discovered my husband-to-be was the third son of King Henry IV of England and uncle to the current one. Well, I thought, if nothing else, that would stop the mouths and the comments of some of the girls I had listened to endlessly! Not one of them appeared to be in line to marry the son of a king, even if it was the king of England and not one of the European royals. I wondered what he was like, would he be old and ugly and infirm like the other husbands I had seen. Was he young, old, ugly, handsome, acceptable?

As if reading my thoughts, my mother said, "you will have a chance to meet His Grace. We are holding a formal engagement ball in two weeks' time. You will have a new set of clothes for the occasion. The wedding will be on the 22nd April."

That was it. I was dismissed. I was seventeen years old and engaged to a man I had never met. Would I be expected to love him? I had no one to answer any of my questions for no one was interested in the small detail of the man himself. For them the only thing that mattered was Jacquetta was marrying a duke. An English duke. A royal. So the talk went and so it was all that mattered.

Feeling lost and scared, I went to the chapel and prayed to the Virgin for help. I asked her to help me love the man I had been betrothed to without my consent or even seeing him, asked her to help me accept the situation and make the most of it, to please my family and my future husband. I asked for my dreams of a lifelong companionship to be made a reality. The Virgin's statue stared back at me, soundless, blank faced, empty. Not a thought or even an impression came into my mind to answer my prayers. I had to believe, oh how much I had to believe, that the prayers had been heard in Heaven and would be answered.

Discreet enquiries and judicious eavesdropping told me my husband-to-be was elderly, to me anyway, being forty something years old, already a widower, his wife having died five months before the marriage he arranged with me. That struck fear into my heart. What if I died in childbirth too? What then of my dreams … but dreams were for children, not for those of us with the responsibility of marriage and households and – what else would I be asked to do, I wondered? I went back to the chapel, to the Virgin and prayed afresh, this time to be allowed to live. This time I caught the flicker of a smile on the Virgin's otherwise blank face, felt the comfort of a touch on my shoulder, knew this time my prayer had been heard. I could relax.

I wholeheartedly committed my days to preparing myself for the great ball whilst thinking about the man I was to marry, persuading myself I was already fond of him and would be a good companion and consort.

It was a tremendous occasion. The room was spectacular, hung with fine silks that billowed into the room from the open windows, drifting on the breeze, creating swirls of colour and light as they did so. There were masses of flowers in huge urns, tables laden with food and others with ale, mulled wine, as well as many other different wines for all tastes. The musicians were the finest that could be found in Luxembourg and the guest list ensured that the cream of society were there.

I made my entrance with my mother, who for once seemed proud of me. All the other occasions had been pretence, I knew that. I knew well that I was a pretty girl, that night my dark hair had been wound up in a mass of curls decorated with pearls and flowers, I had sapphires in my ears, to match the necklace of sapphires my husband-to-be had given me as a gift. They were beautiful. My new gown was cloth of silver slashed with midnight blue, trimmed with Belgian lace. I had new dark shoes with a proper heel. If this was a reflection of life to come, I thought I would be well pleased. I did so like clothes and shoes and jewellery... but then, what seventeen year old girl did not?

My father came over to me and led me across the room, where he introduced me to my husband-to-be. The duke was a good-looking man with deep brown eyes, a ready smile and thick grey hair and beard. Does that sound like a mixture? I was just seventeen, impressionable and vague about what was good and what was not good, despite all the instruction I had suffered during my years. I use the word advisedly. It seems to sum up all that I had endured in the way of endless tuition.

Once the formalities were out of the way, when my parents finally left us to talk, I sat with him and chattered aimlessly. I found him knowledgeable and patient. He told me of his time in France, of the work he had done there, much of which I did not understand at the time. He said how pretty he thought I was and how delighted he was I had consented to marry him. As if it had been my choice... but it was a nice touch and I appreciated that very much.

We danced, he was a good dancer, light on his feet, I found I could follow his lead in almost every dance the musicians played. And so we danced and talked the evening away whilst around me I heard comments such as 'don't they look charming together?' I could not quite believe in love, not at that moment anyway, but acceptance was good. I liked him, I could live with him, I thought. I felt I could be a good companion to him, if nothing else.

At the end of the evening he bowed over my hand, which he held in his much larger one, and asked if we could meet before the wedding, so we could get to know one another better. This was more than I had hoped for and pleased me very much. I agreed and we did, several times he called and we spent an hour or so walking in the gardens or sitting in the fine reception room talking about all manner of things. He told me of his stately home in Rouen which he was sure I would love, of the gardens there and the devoted staff who took care of it all, of the home he had in Belgium, the one he would buy for me in Luxembourg and the one in England. There seemed no end to his estates and properties and I realised I was about to become very wealthy, as his wife. That was good but what was better than that was the fact I liked him very much, in truth liked him more each time he came to see me. I could not wait to be his wife. A small thought crept into my mind that it was an escape from loveless parents and a dull life. Yes, that too was part of it but mostly it was because I liked him a great deal and thought I had done much better in a husband than any of my friends. We did not discuss, but others did, because I heard them, the fact that our marriage had offended the duke of Burgundy, as no permission was sought from him. I wondered why it should matter, but obviously these arrangements were very important to certain people and the duke of Burgundy shunned my husband until his death. Did it matter to me? Not at all. Did it matter to him? He never mentioned it. Why didn't it matter to me is a question I need to answer. Because I thought everyone should be free to marry whoever they wanted. That thought would come back to haunt me several times in my life!

The wedding was a splendid affair, with half the royalty and aristocracy of Europe coming to the ceremony and the celebration. We had so much to do; or rather Mother's staff had so much to do to find lodgings for every single person who had responded to their invitation, lodgings that befitted their status in life. It was not easy ...

The April day was soft, sunny, there were wild flowers everywhere, matching the posy I held. My choice, I had asked for a posy of flowers to match the cream and gold gown my dressmaker had contrived for me. The gown had a low cut neckline which showed my décolletage and made me feel very adult and sophisticated. The pearls my new husband gave me offset it really well. I had a matching bracelet of pearls which I wore over long silk gloves. The day was warm but not that warm and I welcomed both the gloves and the sable cloak he put around my shoulders as we went from one building to another. We were married in the chapel and had the banquet in the Great Hall, as we termed the long room in which we ate, entertained and sometimes had people to sleep. I decided that the weather, the Virgin and fate had conspired to bless my wedding. I prayed for a blessing on the marriage, that I would be fertile and please this charming considerate man who had chosen me out of all the people he could have married, given his position, his wealth and his status in life. I was proud to become the Duchess of Bedford, with all that my new title brought to me, status, wealth, increased standing in the world.

It did not occur to me to think I could have married anyone I chose, not at that time anyway.

It also did not occur to me that our marriage was designed to strengthen the ties between England and the

Holy Roman Empire, as I was cousin to the reigning holy Roman Emperor at the time. I thought myself sophisticated and knowledgeable. I knew nothing. John explained all this to me later and I realised I had been no more than a pawn in the great diplomatic game that was European aristocracy. Did I regret it? No. If I had to have a husband, and obviously I did, no girl/woman could remain unmarried and be of benefit to her family, John of Lancaster was a good choice and a good man. He was gentle and loving and considerate in every way. He taught me the mysteries of the marriage bed and I delighted in it. The only dark cloud was that I did not become with child, despite all my prayers.

We had a magnificent home in Luxembourg and spent our time travelling back and forth between that home, the Belgian one and the one in Rouen, which was the centre of his business life.

There was a momentous trip to England not long after we were married, we visited Coventry and London and had a wonderful time. I loved it and thought, I must return as soon as I can. But back in France we were kept busy being entertained and entertaining those who were important in his career. John had commitments to the king, which he carried out with impeccable charm and ease. He was a natural diplomat and courtier. It was a rich life, a varied and interesting one and I learned a lot about politics, socialising and the way the world views a man of his age married to someone of my age. The men were envious whilst the women pretended to be scandalised at the difference in our ages. I knew it was pretence and I knew too that many of them would have given much to be in my place, either themselves or their daughters. But there was only one Duchess of Bedford at that time, Jacquetta of Luxembourg, star of every occasion, or so John insisted on telling me at the end of every social evening we attended. I would fall into bed with him, be held in his strong loving arms and think I was the luckiest person in Europe. I could have been given to one of the ugly, cruel men I had seen my friends marry. I know I did not look apprehensive when I made my vows, I knew I went willingly into this marriage and I knew many of them did not do the same. I was one of the luckiest people imaginable – at that time. I knew not what the future held, if I had, it would have cast a shadow over a time I look back on with great pleasure.

One thing I learned was how to 'manage' a man so he became what you wanted, not necessarily what he wanted and without him realising it, too. A word here, a hint there and gently but certainly things began to change. At first he did not wish me to travel to Belgium with him, saying the journey was arduous and dangerous but after he had gone to that flat, rather uninteresting country on two occasions without me and I had made a tremendous fuss when he returned, arranging a lavish meal, a decorated bedroom and when he got there, pleasures such as he had not had for a while, he began to see the value of taking me with him, to experience that all the time. And so I began my travels with him. It was a small step but a significant one. My fame began to spread, I was welcomed in many places and John found he could use my influence to help his diplomatic missions. The Virgin seemed to have answered my prayers. I had a good relationship with my husband, even if we were still childless, and I hoped I had found my lifelong companion.

We celebrated our second wedding anniversary in April 1435 by arranging a glorious ball in our home in Luxembourg. We invited everyone who had come to our wedding, we danced and sang and ate and drank and had a wonderful time. We collapsed into bed that night, laughing like young children. He held me close and said, "Jacquetta, whatever happens, this has been a

21

wonderful evening." I didn't know what he meant. I wondered later which dark glass he had looked in to say such a thing. I was afeared of such superstitions. Strange, as it worked out later, how I then hated to have prophesy, signs, even so-called 'wise women' coming to speak to me of this and that. But they fascinated me at the same time and I encouraged them to return. That night, though, I thought he was having foolish fluttery thoughts and told him so.

Sadly, he knew better than I and from that April onward his health began to deteriorate. Flesh fell from his bones, he became gaunt and stiff and virtually unable to walk. I nursed him as best I could, fetched and carried and sat with him and listened to his talk. He told me he feared it was retribution for executing by burning the saintly Joan of Arc, someone he was afraid of at the time but who he had come to realise was a genuine seer. He regretted her death and thought his ill health was due to that. I told him not to be foolish, to put such thoughts away and concentrate on regaining his strength. I bought him broth and herbal concoctions, heated his wine when he said he was cold, persuaded him to eat all that was put before him.

It did not work. He died that September.

Chapter Two

The level of grief a person feels is an indication of the level of affection that person held for the one who has died. I had thought I loved John of Lancaster but I walked around dry eyed and fully in command of my emotions, directing everything from the official mourning clothes to the lying in state and the funeral. No one dared argue with me. I chose the burial place, the priest, the form of elegy at the service and all accepted my words. I knew, from the mirror which hung in our bedroom – I refused to give it up – that black did not overly suit me, it made me look sallow and ill but it had to be. I could always renounce it later, when the mourning period was over. I stared at my reflection, wondering how I could think such things when my husband, someone I admired and was fond of, was at that time lying dead on a bier covered with a cloth and surrounded by candles and flowers.

The answer came in one of those flashes of clarity that are rare but welcome. I had liked him but not loved him. I still had to discover the secret, the heart of that particular emotion. I also realised the Virgin had answered half, but not all, of my prayers. I had not been given a lifelong companion. Two and a half years was not a lifetime. It felt like it, I had done so much, learned so much, experienced so much but the rest of my life stretched before me, however long the Lord God allowed me to live. I was nineteen years old, a rich widow with everything to offer the man who would claim me. But first there were things to do, a funeral to arrange, matters to clear up, houses to sell, estates to organise and dispose of, people to speak to and, God help me, a journey to England to get through.

I had an endless stream of visitors, bringing condolences, papers, problems and gifts, these given in an effort to get into my good graces, I believe. I accepted them all, dealt with them all and got through the funeral in Rouen Cathedral. My black was the best there could be, sparkling with jet to relieve the blackness, if you see what I mean, Spanish lace veil, the whole 'mourning widow' bit in style as only I could do it.

The cathedral was impressive, the funeral was magnificent, the congregation seemingly humbled by the soaring glory of the building. The Requiem Mass filled the space between the stone walls with its heartbreaking solemnity and at one moment I found myself on the verge of tears. I blinked them away under my veil, grateful no one could see them. I had not shed a single tear for John of Lancaster but I missed him by the hour, by the day, his smile, his jokes, his arms, his presence, all had vanished. I even missed the nursing of the sick man, much as it had repelled me at times. I could have allocated a servant to attend to his most personal needs but I took my marriage vows seriously, it was my duty and I did it. He was pathetically grateful for that, which made it impossible for me to withdraw from doing it, even if I had wanted to.

There was a very big hole in my life. It would take a big man to fill it.

When I left the Cathedral, there was a guard of honour waiting for me. I had been aware of the men when we entered, but then I had been following my husband's coffin as it had been reverently carried to its resting place, so I had not looked around at those who were standing in perfect formation at each side of the pathway. I left the Cathedral with my close companions around me, looked at the honour guard and saw, right at the start of the line, one of the most startlingly handsome men I had ever seen in my life. Yes I was young, but I had been to countless social occasions, banquets, receptions, parties of all kinds, but I had never seen a man so good-looking in that entire time. He almost took my breath away. I nodded to the guard and went back to my home. I took a glass of wine and sat in my room, telling everyone I wanted to be alone. Of course they agreed with the request, they had no choice, but no doubt they were thinking I needed to be alone to mourn.

They were wrong.

I spent an afternoon, a whole afternoon sitting in my room, staring out of the window at the landscape which I did not see. All I saw was the face of the man who had been there in that guard of honour, the man who had captured me. I knew two things; one was that I had to find out who he was and the other was that for the first time in my life I knew what love was. There was a third thing, but that was a resolution which came out of the other two things; I had to have him, no matter what it took.

At one point I collapsed onto my bed, not caring that the funereal black was rumpled and that my hair was falling from its many pins and combs. I lay there dreaming, oh how vividly I remember this! To think I never told him about this, either! We talked of a hundred thousand things, that beautiful, handsome, beloved man and I, but I never told him what effect he had on me that day, that funeral day, when my life stopped dead in one direction and began again in a new one. Stopped dead. Oh my, what a connection my mind just made...

What was his name? What was his status? Was he married? Was he available? Was he interested in me? How could I find out without it being obvious? If I showed the slightest interest in a knight, my staff, my family, my companions would immediately try and divert me into the arms of a prince or count or duke or someone. But I knew then, in that long seemingly endless afternoon, that I would not tolerate an old man again. John had been good for me, that I freely admit.

He had taught me much, educated me gently into the arts of love and of being a good wife and consort, he was a good companion, he could dance and talk and keep me in luxury but –

I wanted someone of my age. I wanted someone to be passionate, not gentle, someone who could – dare I even think the word – lead me through my life. It was hard making the decisions; I had found that out when having to arrange everything, from John's funeral to the future of the staff we had in our homes and estates. I wanted an equal. John had been the master, I the little subservient wife, even though I had begun to turn him the way I wanted him to be. It was time to throw off those shackles and tell the world I wanted a man to be equal with me, one to walk with me through the rest of my life.

Most of all I wanted a man to love, completely, wholeheartedly, someone whose presence stopped my breath, someone whose love would surround me and carry me through every adversity. I wanted a man, not a shadow of a man. And I knew too I did not want to walk in the shadow of a man, either. Equality or nothing. That aside, I wanted – whoever that man was.

All I had to do was get him.

I felt guilty. My husband, my loving caring husband who had given me so much, was newly dead and I was already thinking of a successor.

But then, his first wife had died and he had immediately begun to negotiate for my hand in marriage, or certainly within a short space of time. Was it so wrong? I had to have a husband; it seemed no woman could be left on her own.

This time, I decided, *I* would choose to whom I gave the rest of my life.

No one need know I had already made up my mind, if he was free of encumbrances, of course, if he was interested in me, of course.

I sat up, pushed at my tousled hair, pouted at the mirror hanging opposite me and thought to myself, if he was not interested in me as a woman, then he was no man. Something told me otherwise. What I could not say, for he had not betrayed a single flicker of emotion, grief or otherwise, whilst standing guard for me. I just knew it was there.

As it happened, arranging to meet him was easier than I thought. There were affairs to attend to in England. I had to journey there, so I had to have a guard. I did not specify who was to be in that guard, I left that to those in charge of my security, it's what they were paid for, after all. What I did was throw the whole longing and need to know the mystery man into the arms of Fate. I said, 'if he is to be mine, arrange it!'

It was about a week later when the report came to me of who was to be on guard duty. It was a list of their names and responsibilities. I saw the name Richard Wydeville. I knew immediately it was 'him'. I must have seen him in my husband's service, so why had I not noticed how handsome he was, how fascinating he was, how – desirable he was? There, I have said it. A new widow with thoughts of another man. It was shameful, it was guilt inducing, it was – wrong and yet it felt so right. I vowed to confess to some of it and do penance for my thoughts. And wondered why I quantified the confession by thinking I would confess to some of it and not all of it.

Because I was still young, bereft of a husband and therefore at the mercy of the predators who stalked the marriageable widows and young women of the aristocracy I was, at that moment, at the mercy of my own feelings. John had taught me what it meant to be desired and to desire. I had lost that in the last months of his illness, when all I had been able to do was be nursemaid rather than wife. I held those thoughts close

27

to my heart and knew I would not confess to it all. If any of it. It seemed so wrong when thought out in the sanctuary of my prie deu at prayers but not when I was in my bed and thinking of him. Some things I knew were best kept between God and myself without another man intervening and telling me what I could and could not think and feel at this time.

I also knew I would find a way to seek out this Richard Wydeville, find out if he was heart free and wife free and whether he would be an amusing companion for a while. All else could wait until I discovered at least that much.

And so I planned my journey to England – and my life.

It was easily done, as I said. I asked for Richard Wydeville to be brought to me, as I had decided he would be in charge of my security throughout the journey, my time in England and the voyage back. No one blinked, no one hesitated. I was the Dowager Duchess of Bedford and what I said was law, to all intents and purposes. It was influence and power, the very factors I had quickly learned to appreciate during my marriage. Now, with no husband to contradict any of my orders, it was even better.

He arrived in my study some two hours after I asked for him to be brought to me. He was taller than I remembered, with dark brown hair and stunning dark eyes that were full of light, life and amusement. He remembered at the last moment that I was a new widow, gave a deep bow, taking his bonnet from his head as he did so, and offered his sincere condolences. That reminded me, by that fact alone, that he was without an employer because of my husband's death. He had been part of John's contingent of employees, not mine.

"Sire, I have asked you to come and see me as I wish to take you into my employment, if you are so inclined."

He bowed again, with a look of obvious relief. "My lady, it would be a pleasure."

"I wish to know just a little more about you, if you would be good enough to tell me your past history. For example, do you have a wife and family to support?"

He stood, turning the bonnet round and round in his long fingers. I could hardly stop looking at them and wondering...

"No, my lady, I have no wife or family, no commitments that would prevent me from coming into this employ."

"Tell me something of your service."

"I was in command of the forces during the French wars. When I returned to England to serve the king and the duke, I was promoted to Lord High Constable and was made Treasurer of the Exchequer. I am a knight of the Garter."

I had no idea whether being Lord High Constable or Treasurer of the Exchequer was a good thing or not, or how much that elevated him above others, but I knew of the prowess and standing of Knights of the Garter. Adding all these things together, I thought, this is a fine man with a good service record, a good standing in society and – damn it, I want him!

I smiled and shuffled things around on my desk, pretending to be busy. I wondered if he saw through the charade but he stood patiently, waiting for me to speak, without so much as a hint of a smile.

"I have to travel to England to settle some of my husband's affairs," I began, trying to sound efficient and in control, everything I was not. "I would like you to take charge of the arrangements."

He bowed again, this time looking very pleased. "It will be a pleasure."

No, I thought, the pleasure is to come, Richard Wydeville, but not yet. There are certain conventions that have to be observed. But my time – and yours – will come.   Be sure of that.

I asked my husband, some months after we were married, if he remembered the first time he saw me. He said he did. I was a mere chit of a girl, he laughed, trying to look like a sophisticated bride and failing, because my excitement at being married and being created a Duchess was more than I could control at the time. I remembered that feeling well and laughed with him at the memory. He was perfectly correct. He said he saw me often but stayed out of my way for one very big reason, he had fallen in love with me at the moment when I became another man's wife and it hurt, so he tried not to see me. It was pure luck he was placed at the head of the guard of honour that day and said it was all he could do not to stare and try and influence me with his thoughts, his love. He saw my look, saw me assessing him and said his heart leapt, he might have a chance to capture the love of his life. And yes he did see through the charade of my shuffling papers on my desk, but we both knew we had to go through the conventions of society. After all, it was duchess and knight, new widow and those who served her, period of mourning, the whole scenario. And in truth, the mourning was real, for he had lost a fine employer, a man he revered and I had lost a loving caring husband. After the initial euphoria of actually meeting the man I had fallen madly in love with I did collapse into grief. John had been a lovely, darling man and I missed him terribly. But the light on the horizon was the man himself, Richard Wydeville, someone who was free to go with me to England, someone who was prepared to work for me, someone I could – in time, make mine. I had no doubt I would.

Chapter Three

How much Richard Wydeville knew of my plans and dreams at that time? I do not know. We talked of the first impressions, when he saw me, things like that, but I never told him how I schemed and planned to make him mine. I never told him of that long afternoon of guilty pleasure, when I should have been crying and instead was lusting. Give it the right name, that is what I was doing. Once we had that conversation, we never discussed it again, not during our courtship or our marriage, because we always seemed to have too much else to talk about – or do. The only person who had a glimpse into my mind then was my spiritual advisor and confessor and then only in the privacy and confidentiality of the confessional. And even he only had part of the actuality of my feelings. He sympathised, he told me I was young and lonely, that it was natural to desire another man so soon after my husband's much lamented passing and that I should be patient and ask the Virgin to help me through this difficult time. I believe he thought I would lose this feeling and look around for a suitable husband when the period of mourning was over.

He did not know Jacquetta of Luxembourg very well.

Every day Richard Wydeville came to see me, bringing lists, itineraries, suggestions, all for my approval. I left the remainder of the guard to him, arbitrarily picked a date for the sailing, asked him to arrange sufficient provisions for the horses and men, in effect handing over most of the arrangements to him. I told him he was more than capable of dealing with that for me, that I found such things beyond me at that time – here passing a limp hand across my forehead as if in despair at being able to cope in the face of such adversities as a journey to England after being so newly widowed. His face showed his concern and he spoke of his determination to do all he could to help. Talk came back to me, as it always did, of his speaking of me as 'the brave widow taking on the massive burden of the estates and affairs of the duke of Bedford and coping with it remarkably well.' Oh Richard, my beloved man, you had no idea ... the management of John's estates came easy to me, I had helped him a good deal in his work, had sat quietly and listened whilst he spoke with others, so I knew what to do and how to do it.

I wondered, during one afternoon of work, whether John had any premonition of his death, for I seemed to have been tutored in a way to carry on the work by myself. I knew far more, it would seem, than some wives but then 'some wives' are mere tokens. I was more than that to John and I knew I would be more than that to Richard Wydeville, who I knew was caught in my snare, velvet though it might be, snare it definitely was. I wanted him, I got him. It is God's great providence that I was not disappointed in my prize, not for a single moment of our life together.

The voyage to England went unbelievably smoothly. Everything which we needed was stowed on board, nothing got left behind. My ladies were seasick, I was not. I could not understand why the slight swell which carried the ship onward should cause them a problem but perhaps I was made of sterner stuff than they. I was a little upset that I still had to be in black, as did they, for there were beautiful gowns I wished to wear but the official period of mourning was not over and I had to obey the conventions. It did not stop me spending time talking with Richard Wydeville, although we too observed the conventions, always having someone close by when we spoke or walked the deck together. He had much to do to ensure the men, the horses and even the ladies were in good health. He sent a doctor to attend to them when they were sick, fussed over the smallest ailment, knock or bruise they suffered in the alien environment of a sailing vessel. With me he was courtesy itself but his eyes told a different story. Everything I hoped he would be was there in his look sometimes, a deep smouldering fire that longed to break free. I knew it, for I felt the same thing.

England was Autumn, golds and reds, browns and deep dark greens, half bare trees and winds which gusted unexpectedly, bringing a chill to the body and the certain knowledge to the mind that winter was not far away. We stayed in London, were received at court by the king and his courtiers in a most pleasant and welcoming way and had a chance to see some of that famous city, its squalor and its glory. There were many beautiful buildings and parks to walk in. I enjoyed my time, I liked the country and the people. I liked the king very much. I found him to be a man of peace, very handsome in a refined sort of way, quiet of manner, very much in control of himself and his council. I knew he had been king all his life, even if he had been surrounded by advisors and the country run by a regent during his early years. The one thing you recognise immediately is true royalty, it is not a state of mind, it is birth and upbringing, being the descendant of a long line of royal people. Was I not the same?

Business was concluded and we returned to Rouen for the winter. I was sad to leave, for I quite liked the English way of life and the soft landscapes we had ridden through, the grey stone buildings which seemed to grow naturally from the rich soil and the pageantry of the English court. A conflicting set of memories but the abiding one was of Richard Wydeville triumphant in the joust, taking on all comers and winning each time, of his radiant smile as he unseated his last opponent and came riding up to doff his bonnet to me.

"He likes you," one of my ladies murmured in my ear.

"Don't be foolish," I responded, but with a smile.

"He likes you," Maria repeated. "And I'm jealous!"

That pleased me even more. I was young enough to want the man I cared about – and I had to admit that to myself, if nothing else – was desirable in other women's eyes too. It made him more of a conquest. At least, that is the way us women view things. Men may not agree, but what do they know about the way women think, feel and act?

Back in Rouen for the time being – for I had other plans – Richard Wydeville and I took our courtship one step further. He came regularly to my rooms, there to hold me and kiss me and tell me he had never loved anyone so much in his life. I was, truthfully, able to tell him the same thing in return. He consumed my very sleep, my being, my thoughts, my peace of mind. All I wanted was to be married to him, have his children, live where he wanted to live and to give my future to him. He didn't know that within that dream I planned to carefully dictate his future career. I had contacts in the English court and wanted to exploit them. I thought perhaps I could find a place in court, which meant I could use my influence to arrange favours and positions and titles and... He continued to hold back, denying me that which I wanted, his body, saying we had to be legally man and wife. I knew he was right but it was frustrating and infuriating and I often threw pillows and cushions at him when I longed to throw cups, bowls and other breakable things at his handsome face. Then he would trap my wrists in his long fingers and whisper to me of the things we would do when we were married – and then walk out of the room as if he had not a care in the world.

What he did for relief I never asked. I knew what I did, often…

One day, I think just before the Twelve Days of Christmas ended, he arrived with a letter from the king asking that I be brought to England. I had no idea why King Henry VI should want me there, unless he had plans which involved my marrying someone he had chosen, possibly to unite Luxembourg and English aristocracy. That panicked me and we made our plans, hastily putting them into action as soon as we could.

In obedience to the royal summons, we prepared ourselves to leave. The great home in Rouen was closed down, everything was put into store that might be needed in the future, my ladies were given the chance to come with me or remain in Rouen – they all came with me – and we sailed for England in February 1436.

The crossing was rough, this time even I was sick, so we were a pretty miserable group who staggered off the ship and onto dry land, grateful for respite from the appalling seas and howling gale.

We were supposed to go straight to London but Richard and I had other plans. We found a local priest and asked him to marry us, with my ladies as witnesses. They were shocked, for I had said nothing at all to them about it. But they were also thrilled at the love story unfolding before them, because I told them why we were marrying in such haste.

The offer of gold convinced the priest it was the right thing to do so before we went to London, before we showed our faces in court, Richard and I were married.

At the time the fact I was still wearing mourning was not something I took into consideration. No one mentioned it, we just went into this tiny, beautifully decorated chapel with stunning images in niches around the sides and the most delicate painting on the walls and we were made man and wife. Nothing could stop me being the happiest woman in the whole of England at that moment.

As we had told no one of our plans, no one could be forewarned and stop us going ahead with the ceremony. This was my big concern, as I did not know why the king wanted me in England. It was a shock to everyone when we arrived in London and said 'we're married.' The king was said to be furious and refused to see us. We could not do anything but leave my ladies behind, they were welcome, I was not.

Richard held estates in and around Grafton in Northampton, which he had inherited from a half brother, Thomas. We went there, took possession of one of the houses and began our married life. Our first child was conceived there.

Several things happened in quick succession:

First, I discovered my husband was an inventive, considerate and passionate lover, which pleased me very much.

Second, I liked being in England even more than I thought I would.

Third, messages were being carried back and forth between the king and my husband and all became clear. It had been his wish that I came to England as he had taken a liking to me during my previous visit and wished me to be at court. It had nothing to do with any arranging of a marriage, so we were rather hasty, but then again … I was determined no one would have this unbelievably handsome knight. The best way to ensure that was to marry him. So I did.

It was settled, after much discussion, with a hefty fine of one thousand pounds, which we scraped together by selling off some land and making a few cuts here and there … believe me, he was worth it.

When we were able, at last, we travelled to London to present ourselves the king. Being a real part of it, not a visitor, the court was a different place. It was lively but not overly so, there were few banquets and balls as it did not seem to be the king's way of doing things. At that time he had no queen and it did fleetingly cross my mind, was that why he called me to England? Could I have been queen of England had I not fallen in love? I would never know for I could not and would not ask and he would not be undiplomatic enough to say 'had you not married in haste, my lady, you would have been queen.' But the thought lodged in my mind, if I had missed out on the chance of the ultimate position in the land – for a woman – I would perhaps have been able to negotiate a position of equal power for any daughter I might have. At that time I was not aware I was with child. After two years and some months of marriage to John without becoming with child, it did not occur to me that I could become pregnant after so short a time with my new husband. But it didn't matter, for the only man who mattered was there, by my side, legally and eternally mine.

We were at table in the palace with the king that day. Richard was wearing a doublet of deep green slashed with russet and decorated with gold thread. His bonnet, also deep green with a russet feather and gold badge, was on the table by his side. His hair was fresh brushed and shone in the light from the great windows around the hall. His vivid smile flashed across the table at me and I melted, as I did every time he smiled or, in truth, I looked at him. I thought, covering my answering smile with a sip of wine, I am right glad I was not asked to be Queen of England. Oh my husband, my knight, my life, how much do I love you!

The king was a strange man. He didn't seem regal, he seemed – monkish, I think is the only way to describe him. He did not favour elaborate robes, but simple gowns with virtually no trim to them. He spent many hours at prayer, I was told, and attended every service there was to attend. His courtiers had a hard time of it if they were not as devout as he was. He was slender, almost skeletal as if he starved himself although I saw him partake of a hearty meal when we were invited to eat with him. His voice was low and although it carried a degree of authority, he did not have the presence to go with it. He was not an attractive man, his face was long and he favoured a long beard to make it look even longer. His nose was large and his eyes seemed perpetually sad. I wondered what sort of bride he would manage to attract – or negotiate to have – for it seemed odd that he had no queen by his side to help him with the big state occasions and the day to day life of the court. There was so much to do, so many papers to sign, so many decisions to make, surely he needed a helpmeet to work with him. He had shown no sign, or so I was told, of wanting to invite anyone into his life, although there were pressures on him to marry, for the succession of the crown if nothing else.

I am pleased to say we got back into the king's favour. I don't think he was the type to hold a grudge anyway and the hefty fine was compensation enough for our small indiscretion, surely. All we had failed to do was ask for permission. Was that such a big thing? Obviously it was, to him. I blamed the impetuous youth I was. It's a good trick to pull, then no one sees past the conniving person I really am. Sometimes.

Shortly afterwards I realised that I was with child. Richard was delighted. I was more than delighted, for me it was the start of what I hoped would be a big dynastic family. I could see the Wydevilles becoming a major name in English society – if I had anything to do with it.

Richard had many duties in London and often along the coast of England, visiting the ports on various missions for the king. I was always bereft when he went away, so I started going with him. He was concerned at first about my riding long distances when carrying a child but I soon proved I could do it and the exercise was good for me. It enabled me to see parts of England I would not otherwise have seen and I met many people I would not otherwise have met. I was accepted everywhere with seemingly great pleasure and affection. It did Richard's standing a lot of good … not that I would tell him so, not that he would see it that way, men don't, do they? But to see a wife as pretty as me – this is not vanity, this is fact – a dowager duchess to boot, being married to a Knight of the Garter such as the handsome Richard Wydeville, increased his stature in the eyes of others. How did I know this? By their obsequious attitude when they realised who I was. Their attitude went from casual deference to actual respect very quickly. I enjoyed my travels, I wanted to see all of this fascinating country and knew I would go on accompanying my husband as long as I could. As I said, I did not intend to stand in the shadow of a man.

Our child, named Elizabeth, was born in January 1437. She was beautiful. From the moment she came squalling into this world, I thought she was beautiful. Her face was red; she had sturdy limbs and slender fingers which grabbed at everything almost immediately. A mass of black hair completed her looks. I thought she was a miracle, my miracle. From a moment – no, be truthful – a night of lust and love, this perfect being had been created. The red faded fast and the form of her future looks was there for all to see. I took her in my arms and knew I loved her. Into her tiny ear I poured all my wishes for her future, wealth, position, respect, reverence even. And no one, not the midwife or anyone, knew what I was doing. I believed, fervently, that if you wished hard enough and imagined it hard enough, it would happen. I wished my daughter a glittering future and then began wishing for a bigger house. I was sure we were going to have a large family and we would need to accommodate them all.

I knew we would get it, too.

Chapter Four

Our son Lewis arrived a year later. He was small, not deformed in any way but lacking strength in his limbs. I feared for his life the moment he arrived. He was so different in every way from Elizabeth, who was a strong child, strong willed as well. Lewis was baptised in haste, such was the feeling from the midwife and nurse and it was justified. Although he gained in strength for a while, I had my little son for just three months before he went back to Heaven. I was distraught but as I was with child again almost immediately, the grief faded and I spent my time wishing for another son.

Instead of a son, our daughter Anne arrived as the year closed. I could not fully take part in the Christmas revels due to the heaviness of my body but it was a good sign; Lewis had not put such burdens on me. I had ridden and walked and danced until the final month of this pregnancy without discomfort. Anne, like Elizabeth, was a strong child and that put a fear in me that I would not carry sons to grow into adulthood.

I am not the type of person to live with fear, it debilitates me. I had to do something so I asked, discreetly, whether anyone knew of a wise woman I could consult on my future. I needed to know whether I would only bear girls who would live, or whether there would be sons. I could not tell Richard about my fears, he would have laughed them off and told me whatever child arrived was welcome. Yes, they were, but I had plans and dreams for the Wydevilles and sons featured heavily in those dreams and plans. The midwife told me about Clary, a woman who lived in the nearby village to Grafton. I took the midwife's advice for two reasons: one because after my experience with her, I trusted her completely, or I would not have put myself in her hands as I did. It followed that her advice would very likely be right. Two, she had consulted this Clary person herself and found her accurate and helpful.

When I was at last able to go out, I arranged to visit Clary.

I rode to the village one Spring afternoon, with the sun dappling through the new leaves, a scattering of wild flowers in the grass along the verge, riding along thinking life could not get any better, not at that moment anyway, knowing I was deliberately blocking out the thought that the woman would tell me I would not bear sons.

We had been given directions to her home and the armed guard led me there unerringly. We went through the village and down a narrow pathway, almost out the other side of a small wood. The cottage was ramshackle, just as I thought it would be, clean, the bundles of herbs hanging from the rafters the only sign that the woman's home was the place to come for potions and pills. She was not very old, although she had some grey hairs showing under her white cotton cap. She had a calm face with near perfect skin, clear blue eyes, a small nose and lips that seemed to be eternally ready to smile without quite making it. I thought she was pretty and wondered if she had admirers. Her gown was old, worn in places but clean with a white apron overlaying it, tied in a huge bow at the back. She had leather shoes on, laced with long thongs tied in neat bows. She seemed to like bows; the herbs were tied that way, too.

Clary had known of my coming, as I had sent a messenger to ask if it was all right, so she may have put everything away to make the place tidy for me. There was a comforting smell in the cottage of wood ash and herbs, soap and even the scent of flowers, although there were none to be seen.

It was the first time I had been in a villager's home and it surprised me how small it was. Why I should be surprised I had no idea, perhaps I thought –

no, even now I cannot say what I thought. What I did realise was, this was a level I would never wish to sink to. Everything had to be done to prevent the Wydevilles from ever living in a place like this. By 'like this' I mean a two-roomed cottage, with beams and thatch which did not look entirely waterproof, a door that allowed draughts to circulate and a fire that could have done with some larger logs. I glimpsed a bed through the open doorway to the other room and saw blankets that did not look half as thick as those I had on my bed. I vowed then if the message I received was favourable, I would send her some furs or comforters for the winter months. Then I thought that was unfair, it would not be her fault if the message was not favourable, so I decided to send the furs anyway. There was a scrubbed table in the middle of the room and two stools either side of the hearth. The floor was earth beaten down hard and looked as if it had been swept. There were no rugs. I saw shelves with an array of bottles and bowls on them. I was intrigued and wished I could look around more without appearing rude.

"My lady." The curtsy was not as practised as those I was used to but it pleased me anyway. "I am honoured you have come to see me."

"I seek information," I told her. "You were recommended to me."

Clary gestured to one of the stools and I carefully sat down, trying without success not to allow my skirts to trail on the floor and wondered why. It didn't matter, it was no more than dust which I found in my own home at times. There was nothing to harm me. We were alone, the guards were outside, the door was closed, no one could hear us. I wondered why that was important. I realised I was thinking wildly, as if touched with panic. I did ask myself if I was sensible to be there, Richard would surely laugh at me when he found out. I didn't want that to happen.

"Tell me what it is you wish to know." As she spoke, I noticed she had changed, she had aged in a moment, there were lines where she had none before. The eyes looked older, more solemn. It was as if someone had taken the young woman's place, or that she had aged in a few heartbeats. I was scared for a moment but the voice, which had also changed and had become deeper and slightly rougher, sought to console me. It was the voice of an old woman, far older in years than the one I had come to see.

"I am the guardian of this one. Fear not. I speak through her and when you leave, my lady, she will remember nothing of what has been said."

Fear grappled with sense for a few breaths, who was this, what was this, but the thought that Clary would not remember anything was in itself a consolation. I held a tiny fear she would talk of me in the village. Why I had that notion I don't know, my midwife had not said she was a chattering woman. I took a deep breath and said what was in my heart.

"I have given birth to two healthy girls and one boy, who died too soon. My fear is I will not carry a boy child who will live. Can you tell me whether this is so, or whether my future sons will be healthy."

There was silence in the cottage for a few moments, apart from the soft sound of ash falling in the hearth. From outside I heard the clink of harness as the horses grazed, the murmur of the voices of the men as they talked and enjoyed the sunshine, the call of birds darting from tree to tree. It was as if all my senses were sharper, I even felt the blood surging round my body in response to my heartbeat and I became aware of a new life inside me, too. That was a secret I would keep for a while longer, I thought.

Then Clary spoke. She sat up straighter, staring at me but not seeing me. The same older, rougher voice spoke to me.

44

"You have new life in you now. This one will also be a girl. Fear not, my lady, the sons will come. Not as many as you would wish but there will be healthy boys. The son to come before too long will be a shining star in the firmament. His name will live on forever for the deeds he will do and the work he will achieve. There will be others. But put not the girls to one side, my lady. The one you have already, the child of your heart, your firstborn, is destined to be a greater shining star than your son. I see great things for you – for your family, but I also see great heartache too. No one can live without heartache. It is the lot of human life.

"You carry many dreams and wishes, my lady, for the future of your family. For a while they will be fulfilled. Hold not to the adventurer son who is to come, for he will make his way in the world on his terms, not yours. Hold not to the girls who marry for they must make their lives with their husbands. Hold fast to the man you love for he is everything to you and I say you to him, too. A love as huge as that needs to be cherished and I know well you cherish it – and him.

"Our words are meant to guide, my lady, to guide only. Ever do you have the freewill to go your own way, do what you think best for your family. But remember our words."

In that moment the strange older 'look' vanished and Clary became herself again, blinking and smiling shyly at me.

"Did you get your answers, my lady?"

"I did. Thank you. Can you tell me what happened?"

She looked down at her hands, work-worn and older than the rest of her. "When someone comes to ask me a question, one that is from the heart, people come from the other side. They speak through me; I have no memory of their words. But I know what they say is right."

45

I wanted to know who 'they' were but I also wanted to assimilate the words, the message I had been given, to write it down so I didn't forget any of it. If I began a discussion with Clary on how and where, I would lose the words.

I got up and felt in my purse for a coin. It was a gold one. I hesitated and then gave it to her anyway. She looked at it and gasped, her eyes wide with shock. She held it out to me but I waved it away.

"My lady, that is too much."

"I have other questions, not of what I was told, but how it was conveyed to me. Clary, please accept the coin and tell me, may I return and ask my questions?"

"If it pleases you, my lady." She bobbed her head and gave me that small curtsy again. "Whenever it suits you. No need for a message, just come. I am rarely far from home. And thank you very much for the money." She did not ask why I did not give her my questions there and then. It was as if she knew. She opened the door for me and I went to pass through, then stopped. There was one thing I had to ask, one that could not wait until the next time.

"When I came in, I smelled flowers, but there are none here. Why did I smell flowers?"

She looked at me very sharply then, her head tilted to one side. "Flowers? That is a scent that comes before I am used to give a message. I thought I was the only one who could smell it. My lady, you need to come again to talk to me. There is much for us to discuss."

I felt a chill go down my spine at her words. I suddenly thought, did I have an incipient talent for this work too? Would it be possible, was it possible, could I-

"I will return," I told her and saw her answering smile. She said nothing else. The men were ready to get going when I went out into the sunshine; my head was reeling with what I had seen and heard. We rode back home and I swear I was not aware of a thing the whole way. I might have been asleep for the entire journey from what I can remember of it.

But I do recall going straight to my study where I wrote down everything I had seen and everything I had heard. My heart skipped several beats when I wrote the words 'for a while they will be fulfilled' but that too was part of life. What is built up must at some time come down again. I could ignore that for the time being and concentrate on the remainder. I would have sons, the ghost/spirit person said so. My sons would do great things. The Wydevilles were going upwards, of a surety.

I also knew I wanted to return to Clary fairly soon, for I felt a kinship there. I longed to know so much, who these people were, how one spoke with them, how one received their wisdom, their guidance, their friendship. I wondered how I knew there would be friendship, too.

The strange thing is, none of it felt strange. That is a complete contradiction but it is true. It was strange to me that I did not find it strange. It was natural. I went to a person, they assumed the persona of another, older, possibly dead person and they gave me the answer to my questions. Clary just took a deep breath and that person was there. It was that easy for her. Would I be able to learn to do that? I thought perhaps not, for who would be there to listen to the words given through me if I did? I needed another way of looking into the future; a way that allowed me to see for myself what was to come. I had much to discover.

"We will learn more," I told my reflection, for she and I understood one another well. Neither of us told secrets about the other and we both held silent and still that which we knew. "We will learn more and we will – learn to do the same, perhaps."

The thought was scandalous and tantalising, the concept intriguing and terrifying. I knew I would go back and I felt Clary was waiting for me to go back, too.

The only thing I had to decide was how much to tell Richard. In the end I told him everything. I expected him to laugh, to scorn the message, to tell me I was stupid to pay someone for such rubbish. He did none of those things. He sat quietly and listened, never interrupting once, not even when I said I wanted to return and see what I could learn, as I felt I had a talent for the 'work, if it could be called that.

"If you wish to learn, my beloved one, then go. I would never stop you doing what you wanted, you know that."

"That doesn't tell me if you approve or disapprove."

"I'm not ready to know if I approve or disapprove!" He smiled and as always I simply melted at the sight. "I don't know enough to say the woman is a fraud, that she managed to persuade you to give her money-"

"No!" I interrupted. "She asked for nothing at all, not before or after. I gave it freely."

"Apologies. Maybe she did not, then. Maybe she is genuine. You will only know if you go back and you learn from her and she proves to you and to me that you have a genuine talent. Then I will know she is genuine, too. Is that a fair statement, beloved?"

"It is and I thank you for it. I truly thought you would laugh at me."

"That I would never do. You never do anything without due consideration and you gave this every consideration before you went. I have to say it has done some good, for the shadow I saw around you has lifted."

Shadow? Had it been that obvious? He must have seen my expression for he took my hands and then pulled me close, kissing me tenderly. "My dear, dear wife, only I know how much the loss of our son meant to you and how much you long for sons to carry on our name. I am not surprised you sought guidance on the subject. I am glad you did, for I see you lighter and happier now. Before the son you want comes, give me another daughter, I beg you. I love them."

And I did.

My daughter Jacquetta – well, why not? It is a good name, after all – came into this world strong, healthy and shouting even louder than the others. Another daughter for the dynasty I was fast building. Richard was pleased, as he had said he would be, but I still longed for my son, the one who would carry on the Wydeville name, inherit the Wydeville fortune I was sure we were going to make and if I had not had the words of the wise woman's 'guardian', whoever she was, I would have been most unhappy at Jacquetta's birth. Instead I took this one into my arms and told her she was beautiful, loved and needed and that she had a glittering life ahead of her.

It was wrong of me, in many ways, to be disappointed. Jacquetta was a wonderful child to have, pretty and talented in many different ways. She brought joy and happiness to us all and she made a very good marriage. There, I have said it, I was wrong to be disappointed at her birth, even though the guardian had told me I would bear another daughter. I am admitting it now, although I told no one of my feelings at the time. Really I should have concentrated on being grateful for healthy children, so many families, of high and low rank, lost their newborn and young children regularly, through all manner of illnesses and accidents. Mine, mostly, thrived.

I went to see Clary as soon as I was able to leave home after Jacquetta's birth. There is this tiresome convention that a woman has to be isolated for so many days, then attend church to be 'cleansed' as if giving birth is some disgusting thing. She has to have men kept

49

away from her, which makes me mad but I have to go along with it for anything else would cause scandal and I thought I would be doing enough of that by visiting Clary, among other things…

Autumn had come sooner than expected, there had been a good harvest which had been gathered in early and stored and now the leaves were busy throwing themselves under the horses' hooves, so they made a satisfying crunching sound as we rode. I confess to loving Autumn best of all, I love the colours, the clear skies, the crispness of the days and the coolness of the nights. We had a small cart with us loaded with wood and two thick furs for Clary's bed. I hoped she would be pleased. The firewood was an afterthought, as I remembered thinking she needed large logs which would burn longer. I hoped I would not overwhelm her with the gifts, the furs were not strictly needed and as for the firewood, I had servants enough to chop more for our use.

Clary did not know we were coming this time but the cottage looked the same as it had before, tidy, clean and sparse. She dropped that small curtsy when she saw me, then her eyes widened when she saw the firewood being unloaded and gasped in surprise when one of the men handed her the furs. She held out a hand and took mine, leading me into the cottage.

"My lady…" She had no words of thanks. I waved a hand toward her.

"I wanted to do something for you. No thanks are needed. I come with a request."

"Do you wish answers again, my lady?" She held the furs in her arms, obviously relishing the softness of the skins.

"Not answers such as I had last time, answers on how it works, who comes to speak and – can I learn to do it?" There. It had been said.

Clary sat down on her stool, still clutching the furs as if they would escape or someone would take them from her.

"I know I said we must talk again, but ... you, my lady, want to learn..." She said this in a faint disbelieving voice. "But you are..."

I sat down opposite her. "What am I, Clary?"

"One of-"

"One of 'them? One of the ruling class, someone who goes to London and talks with the king?" She nodded. "I am still a woman, still have feelings, still have questions and still want to know things. Like, who spoke to me, how does it work, can I learn to speak with such people, guardians, spirits, ghosts, whoever they are? It interests me, no, that's not entirely true; it's more than that. I must be honest with you. It's a need in me to know."

The men were making a good deal of noise outside as they unloaded the logs into the small overhang where Clary stored her firewood. I heard the sound of something scuttling just beyond the wall, no doubt the logs had disturbed whatever it was. Clary remained silent for a few moments and I wondered what she was thinking.

Then she looked me in the eyes properly for the first time. "That was the word I needed, my lady, need. I was not going to help you if it was just an interest, for those who speak with those beyond the veil of life have to do it with seriousness, not for play, not for fun, not for interest."

She spoke with the assurance and diction of someone above her station. It was obvious she had spent a lot of time speaking with those 'beyond the veil,' as she put it. I could learn well from Clary, if she would but teach me. I held my breath for a moment, wondering if she would still refuse.

"I am offering money for the tuition," I said when she remained silent.

"Money will be welcome, it always is, but I will not do it for the money, my lady. It has to be a gift, not a payment. The work of the spirit world is not done for coin but for love. I have to repeat this: it must be done seriously. We do not play, nor do the spirits we contact when we wish to work, to serve them."

"I understand. So be it."

"How strong was the scent of the flowers when you came to see me?"

The question took me by surprise. I thought for a moment. "When I came in, I smelled herbs, woodsmoke, ash and fresh flowers. I looked round for them, thinking you might have brought them into the house because I was coming, but there were none to be seen."

She smiled. "A strong scent, then. You are ready to learn, my lady. Of every person who has come to me, not one has smelled the flowers. Not one. And not one of them has asked to learn how to do these things, to contact those who are gone before us." She stood up. "Come and see me at the turn of the month, my lady, at the time of the new moon. We will commence our work on that date."

I stood up and took her roughened hand to seal the bargain. "Turn of the month. I will be here."

"I thank you from my heart for the fuel and the furs. They will serve me well this coming winter."

"It is a small thing for me, I am glad to give it."

We had no more to say to one another. With pounding heart I left, already counting the days to the turn of the month and a secret to learn.

Chapter Five

I was grateful I had the message safely recorded, in my heart as much as anywhere else, for my next child, a boy, lived only a very short time. If I recall rightly, it was about two weeks before my son John was interred in his tiny grave. I mourned him but sent his spirit back with a mother's love to the world from which he came. By then I had progressed a long way, with Clary's help. She was very advanced in her knowledge and skills, much of which she kept to herself. I think I was the only person who knew the extent of her powers.

She taught me how to calm myself, to see pictures and believe as well as interpret what I saw, taught me scrying with a bowl of water or a dish of sand. I learned how to look into the future and understand what I saw, as sometimes it came as a vision rather than a clear message. Other times the message was as clear as the water I looked into and I watched it change and swirl and reveal its secrets to me. There was talk, of course there was, that I was learning witchcraft but Clary and I laughed this off and said we shared 'woman talk'. No one believed it, we were worlds apart in our social standing but it served as a veil for what we really did. I learned how to serve them as well as they serving me, it was not a one way thing, nor should it be. I often received words to send healing to someone I knew and this I did. I would be prompted to go and visit someone, to find they needed comfort or counselling and again, this is what I did. No one knew, it was often said 'how did you know I needed someone right now?' which pleased me muchly. Even as I served the spirit world, they in turn were serving me, for it added to my reputation as someone who cared. Not that many people seemed to care, it was a very selfish time. I learned about herbs suitable for various illnesses and that too became something I used a lot in my life. It was invaluable, all of it.

Richard encouraged me in all I did. He was eager to know what I had learned every time I went to Clary and tried to help but he was behind a barrier of his own making. Because of that, he could not 'see' anything. I tried hard to get him to meditate, as I thought our joint power would take us to higher levels but he was incapable of quieting his mind or even giving the time to just sit with me. He was impatient and demanding, if it did not happen immediately then he would not wait. Typical man, wanting to be jousting or practising or riding or hunting rather than sit quietly and see what the spirit world had to tell him. So I just told him what I had learned, in the sanctuary and peace of our marital bed, watched his face alight with interest and then, when I suggested he try again to work with me, watched the interest fade and he begin to talk of the new hunter he had acquired, the new way of fletching arrows, the new anything but his efforts to sit in the quiet with me. So a pattern was established, I did the farseeing, he did the listening and that suited us both.

In 1441, I think it was, we acquired the rights to the manor house known as The Bury and moved in. At last we had room, a chance to spread out, just as I had always known we would. It was a handsome house with extensive grounds, enough space for our growing family. I was with child again and I knew that this time I would have the son I craved, for all the signs were right. I had seen it in the scrying bowl, seen my son being baptised. I even knew his name. Antony. I named him before he was born for St Antony of Padua, thinking that would be a good omen for him.

Richard was in France with the duke of York much of that year so, with great pleasure, I oversaw the move to The Bury. It was my dream to have a large place and to be able to direct the move myself made it even better. My Seneschal helped, of course, doing the actual ordering of the staff, but the instructions came from me. What a flurry of packing and sorting and discarding and buying new there was at that time! I loved it, every moment of it. I kept a stern face on, though, so none would know of my intense pleasure and take advantage of it. Servants need to be controlled, as much as children do. My children were into everything then and their nursemaids had a real task holding them back from getting lost or hurt in the move.

They loved the new home and the freedom it gave them to run, ride and play when not at their lessons. I insisted on lessons for them from an early age, just as I had. I needed them to learn manners to the point when it was ingrained in them, then they could not make a mistake in the future. I made sure their tutor had a strap handy, just as mine had. I found children learned better when they were avoiding punishment. Cruel, maybe, but I had plans for them all and they had to conform to that which I wanted, good manners, good education, good behaviour. I would not tolerate anything less. My upbringing had ensured that I had all those things. I wanted the same for them, the girls as well as my sons. When they arrived. I insisted they learned deference to all who were above them in rank. I just knew it would be needed one day.

I was with child again and had a completely trouble free pregnancy. In June of 1442 Antony, my golden son, came into the world with no problems at all. As if to match the birth of this much longed for son, Richard was created Knight Banneret, a great honour, and was made Captain of Alencon at the same time. It would seem the king thought highly of my husband – nearly as highly as I did.

I was able to go to London for a time, to mingle with the courtiers and the many women who flocked around the court, bright butterflies, every one of them. I studied their fashions, their speech and their mannerisms and decided I had to alter nothing of the way I was. It is limiting when one has to consider every word before it is spoken; it takes away the confidence and the ease with which you associate with people. I was glad I had nothing to fear from these women, apart from the usual jealousies and envies that accompany any group of females when put together. That is, ignoring the fact I outranked them all at that time. It pleased me muchly that I was known firstly as the dowager Duchess of Bedford, the title still rang like a bell in my ears and secondly as 'the widow who entrapped the most handsome man in England.' Now that really did ring like a bell in my ears and I was mightily glad Richard and I married when we did, for there were quite a few ladies who would have done their best to turn his face in their direction had they been given the chance. I wondered then which of my helpers had been watching over me to ensure that I made the right decision at the right time and that he acquiesced, so that we were safely married before we entered London.

My helpers. Yes, by then my connection with those on the other side of the veil was an integral part of my life. I could sense them, hear them, speak with them without anyone knowing. I had what Clary called guides, a beautiful wise calm nun in a traditional habit, an abbess in fact, who spoke to me gently of womanly things and helped me in many ways. She guided me with my children when they were ill or hurt in some way. I knew as much or more than the resident physician, whom I kept on just for appearance's sake, and to treat the servants. My children and my husband I treated myself if they needed it. The physician would look at me in astonishment when they recovered quickly from whatever ailed them and would often ask what I had used. I would tell him and he would shake his head, and say things like, "That would never work." This despite the fact the living proof was in front of him.

One of my helpers was a cleric, Father Nicholas. I sensed him as an extremely old man with so many wrinkles in his face it would be hard to see the man he had once been. I adored him; his quiet gentle funny ways amused me considerably. He had a sharp eye for the humorous and would often whisper comments to me about the people I was speaking with. I had to learn to control any laughter he induced for fear of being considered a little mad. I relied on his wisdom to help me with the men in my life, from my husband to the servants and hired hands. It seemed to work well, I ran an efficient, friendly and happy household.

I also had someone with me who was more angelic than anything. I looked on that one as my guardian, keeping me from harm. With these helpers I was more than content to explore the future in a guarded way, being careful of what I asked, not presuming on their goodness and asking for that which I could not achieve by hard work and my own guile.

This will seem like a litany of births but – well, I suppose it is. We had been busy making up for lost time, if you know what I mean. Richard's tenure in France with the duke of York had kept him from our bed for too long. Mary arrived the year after my beloved golden son. She was a dark haired, dark eyed beauty who won all our hearts from the moment she arrived. My bold son John came next. Unlike his namesake he thrived, grew taller than any of my children and was strong in every way. He was a fearless fighter from an early age. Somehow I knew he was not destined to make old bones – and he didn't but he lived every moment of his life to the full. Few people can ask for more than that. But I admit here that his death broke my heart, he was a favoured son. It is unfair of any mother to have favourites but when you have as many children as I did, with a great proportion of them living, too, it is hard not to have favourites. Every child was an individual, some were more likeable than others, as you find in any group of people. My task was to love them all the same, work for all of them the same, plan their futures and leave them to make of what I gained for them in their hands, to hold or throw away as they saw fit. I could do just so much.

That brief overview of my ever-growing family took me to the year 1445.

I say it as if it was a momentous year and it was. That was the year Henry VI married Margaret of Anjou in a glittering ceremony in Hampshire.

The negotiations had gone on and on and for a while we thought nothing would happen, it would all fizzle out and he would remain without a queen and wife, but finally it had been arranged. Margaret of Anjou became wife and Queen Consort to Henry VI and England had a marriage and later that year a coronation to celebrate. We were invited to the wedding and, later, to the coronation.

I was not carrying. Thanks be to God I was not with child at that time, although how this miracle occurred I do not know. I thought it was going to be a child a year regardless … but that year I managed to avoid it and so I could order beautiful tight fitting gowns for both occasions. For the wedding I chose a mauve that was two shades away from royal purple, embroidered with seed pearls and set with lace on neckline, sleeves and hem and for the coronation I chose ivory, embroidered with gold thread depicting the lily of the valley, my favourite flower. No lace this time, just masses of gold thread so the gown glittered as I moved. I could not make up my mind which one I liked most.

Margaret of Anjou was amazingly pretty. She had calm features that hid most of her thoughts; I only learned in later years to look for the tightening of the lips or the merest crinkle around the eyes to detect her bad moods. She had them, for sure, moods as black as the most inner recesses of a hearth. They would swoop down on her in a blink of an eye and the smiling laughing person would become straight faced with the tell-tale tics of temper revealing themselves only to those who knew her well. The others suffered the consequences of not knowing by continuing the foolishness or whatever it was that sparked the bad mood. But that was in the future, when I was in constant attendance on her as one of her favourites, says she with a nonchalant air. Let no one think I aspired and conspired to get there … of course I did! How else did I get in that position? It was the perfect place to promote my family, which is all that interested me. No, that drove me, I have to be honest.

The big showy wedding made me wish for a moment or two that I had been able to have such a ceremony with half the world looking on but I knew one thing, even as I watched the couple walking together from the church, this was not a love match as mine had been, this was an arranged alliance. All the glitter and gold and high-ranking guests imaginable do not make a good marriage if it is not based on love. Richard and I might have had a hasty wedding but our relationship was one rooted solidly in love, he for me and me for him. No other man exists for me but my husband – then and now. I could - and did - trade the glitter and gold for the love which made my heart soar every single day, whether he was with me or not.

There is one thing I have to say here. I had not, up to that moment, seen what Clary referred to as 'auras', the outline of someone in light and colour. She had tried hard to show me the auras of living things, of herself, but

I failed to see them. That is, until the day of the wedding of the king of England and Margaret of Anjou. As they stood in the doorway of the church and awaited the cheers and applause of the gathered multitude, I saw, for a fleeting instance, Margaret's aura and it chilled me, for it was red. I did not know then of her temper and rages but the aura showed it clearly and forewarned me. I looked at Richard standing alongside me and his aura, which I had never seen before, was gold. The difference was amazing. I brooded on it for some time and decided I had to speak to Clary about this the next time I went to see her. I was quietly happy that I had seen an aura, after all Clary's hard work in trying to show me how to do it. I thought she would be pleased.

We did talk about it and she told me to watch out for anyone whose aura bothered me in any way. It was a warning I took seriously. I did not see auras all the time, I decided later that I could only see them when something had heightened my senses, such as the wedding and coronation, great events like that. Day to day, I did not see them. It would have helped if I had, but then again, I had enough to look at and concentrate on, the way people looked when speaking, working out if they were lying or not, whether the words meant one thing and their intent was another, watching their hands, their body, did they twitch with lies, or stand passive and speak the truth, that kind of dissection. All part of court life. I hoped my children learned enough to be able to be in court and not be caught out by anyone. It was not easy; everyone had their own ideas of what they wanted and how to get it, even if it meant trampling on someone to get it. For many, the need, the desire, the burning ambition to get whatever it was they had set their heart on meant they had no scruples about bringing others down as they aimed for their goal. I know well there were many who held that opinion about me but they were wrong. I worked for what I and my family had, without once bringing anyone down. I defy any one of them to name someone injured – mentally or physically – by my actions.

The royal wedding was like any other, only on a grander scale. Musicians, minstrels, tumblers, jugglers, all came to entertain as we ate and drank, then there were stately dances and a good deal of ale flowing everywhere. Richard and I left as soon as we could politely do so, fortunately the gathering was extensive enough that no one would notice if we slid quietly away, which we did. I knew my beloved man had been bored, such occasions did not please him overly unless there was jousting or tourney in which he could take part. There was none at the wedding but there was jousting aplenty after the coronation. And as always he excelled at the joust, winning many of his contests. I had visions of my sons learning to ride that well, to joust that well, to hold their own in court and was surprised at the glow I felt when I thought on it. I hadn't realised fully how much it meant to me until that moment.

That was a great spectacle of flamboyant decoration, music, dancing, wine flowing for the populace, food distributed to the poor, everything a Coronation should be. I would have been very pleased to be there for but one thing. As the cup was placed in Margaret's hands during the ceremony, I saw them dripping in blood. The sight chilled me and I actually shivered to the point when Richard asked if I needed his mantle. I said no, it was just a goose walking over my grave. I told him later what I had seen and he was not surprised. "That woman is trouble," he said seriously, when we talked about the occasion.

"I fear for Henry," I said, without knowing why.

"She will control him completely," Richard said with quiet surety. I was beginning to wonder if he had the ability to contact the spirit world after all but then realised it was his own reading of the woman who had come to be the centre of our lives. He was right, too, in every way. There could hardly be a more unsuitable choice of Queen Consort for the quiet pious meek man we had as our king at that time. But we had to live with it – and the new Queen – for Margaret had singled me out during the days of celebration following the wedding. I was the other 'foreigner' in court and we had much to talk about – and did. I cannot say for a moment I liked her, she was useful to my plans and anyway, you did not reject the Queen's request for you to be with her, it wasn't politic to do so. I knelt by her, stood by her, sat with her, on a lower stool, of course, helped her with tapestries, the endless tasks women do, stitching for hours on something to hang on the wall knowing no one will notice it anyway and talked about court, the people she had to deal with, giving her their background so she could make up her own mind whether to trust them or not. That was something she had to decide, I was not going to commit myself to any statements like that, knowing well they could rebound on me.

I found I could tolerate being with her, provided I had some time away. This I did by becoming with child again. When I was about six months through the pregnancy and very large, I felt myself too ungainly to be in court and was longing for the peace of Grafton. The Queen gave me permission to go home for the remainder of my pregnancy but told me to hurry back as soon as I had been churched.

I was grateful to be back in the home I loved. I was grateful to be out of the spotlight, for it felt as if everyone was staring at me all the time. I asked myself, was it because I was not English, because I was prettier than the women who were there, because I had the most handsome husband in the country … what was it, or was it entirely down to my suspicious mind and no one was actually staring at me after all?

It mattered not one jot. I had time away from court, time to be with my fast growing daughters, to enjoy their progress and the development of their amazingly beautiful faces. I knew they would all be beautiful and that pleased me. Richard was incredibly handsome and I was pretty, we should have produced beautiful children but there were always throwbacks somewhere, ancestors who were not as handsome or pretty and a child might not be as goodlooking as I hoped. So far, though, they all were and I had to pray that it would continue to be that way.

My son Lionel arrived in 1447. He was another strong, vigorous child I knew instinctively would live. He was a handsome boy from the very start and I marked him down for Great Things. It was a relief to find the original prophesy had been fulfilled. I occasionally had a twinge of worry when I recalled that my dreams would be fulfilled only for a while, but I put it to one side and determined to enjoy that which I had.

Richard, riches and the favours of the new queen of England. Even if it did come at a price. My aching knees, for one.

We were Lancastrian supporters, of course. Richard was employed by Lancastrian royalty and aristocracy so there was no question of where our loyalty lie. Or so I thought. When I looked into the scrying bowl one night when all were sleeping and no one could break my concentration, I saw the Lancastrian arms breaking apart, dissolving into nothing. It worried me, for there was our future fame and fortune. I spoke with Father Nicholas and he said yes, it would so break but I had nothing to fear. All would be well. I trusted him and put the concern aside.

Another night I saw the king knighting my husband. I had thought for some time, that an earldom would be nice. I had mentioned it in passing to Margaret, in the hope she would be smart enough to take my hint and pass it on. What name to choose … I pondered on that for a time, in secret, as I did everything which related to the future. No one knew my dreams, schemes and plans apart from the spirit people around me. Richard was not privy to all my thoughts. Why give my dreams to a man to carry when I could work on them myself? He had enough to do simply being Richard Wydeville, husband, father, knight, estate manager, king's envoy… he needed nothing else to occupy his thinking time.

A name. Why not ask, I thought? So I did and was given the vision of a river. An odd vision. I thought about it for a while, wondering what it meant, how it related to being an Earl, until I said 'Earl Rivers' out loud and realised it sounded right. I stored it for the future, vowing to mention it to Richard one night after love, when he was most receptive, as men usually are. I also vowed to pass that piece of wisdom on to my daughters…

Talking of whom, Katherine arrived in 1448, blonde, beautiful – as all my daughters were – and a joy to have. I had to hurry back to London as soon as I could after her birth, as there was a momentous occasion to celebrate. My husband was elevated to the rank of Earl and became the 1st Earl Rivers. I have to say, when someone asked him where he got the idea for the name, he just said 'it sounded right.' That was the truth but no one, no one knew where it had come from. It was something I whispered in the middle of a passionate night, as I had planned, and hoped it had registered. Obviously it had. I was very pleased.

There was no one in the land happier than I was that day. Everything I had worked for was coming together. All my work, my contacts, my influence, my sacrificing time with my children to be in London, to be at the centre of the policy making, money possibility, court, was paying off. My husband was an Earl. My daughter Elizabeth was maid of honour to Queen Margaret. I had another beautiful daughter for the Wydeville dynasty. I had a firm foothold. It was all I wanted – at that time.

Chapter Six

Despite a few problems at home, such as my daughter Martha arriving and only living for a few hours, and at court, where there were rumours about the king's mental state as at times as he seemed to lose touch with reality, life continued on its usual course. I kept my heartbreak over Martha to myself. It was not something I could share with the Queen and in any event, I was soon breeding again. The problem was, the Queen was not, much to her annoyance.

"It's not for want of trying," she told me one day, almost in tears. I do mean 'almost', she never gave way to such 'weak' emotions in public. I knew Margaret was worried about her husband, not out of love for I doubt she knew the meaning of the word, but for what it meant to her as Queen Consort. It didn't stop her policy-making efforts, she knew what she wanted from life and, like me, was determined to get it. She wanted to know how I could produce such a large family. I longed to say 'because our marriage is built on love and passion' but that would not have gone down well. I just said I was fortunate to be so fertile. It didn't pacify her, though.

Our daughter Eleanor arrived in the same year that Elizabeth was married to Sir John Grey, a staunch Lancastrian supporter with his own estates and wealth. Although sad to see the first of my brood leave the Bury, as I was busy adding to the ever-growing crowd, it was also a relief. Elizabeth had done well in her time in court, learned many things, including the art of being a good wife. John Grey was a pleasant quiet man who would be a good husband to her. I was pleased with those negotiations and thought she had made a good match.

My visions and the scrying bowl showed me children and happiness and then went black. I could see no further than that. Sometimes it seemed the future was shielded from us for our own good.

Antony was growing into the handsome man I foresaw, he was excellent at jousting, good at all his lessons, pious, proud, ambitious, everything a Wydeville should be. I was so very proud of him.

Everything in life seemed good, especially when Margaret proudly announced she was with child. At last, the cherished wanted heir was to arrive! But, as if to offset the happiness of that announcement, Henry went into some kind of breakdown, fugue, call it what you will. For a year he knew nothing, but we did.

Richard, duke of York, was appointed regent.

Imagine, a York taking control of a Lancastrian court and country! Rumours began to fly, of course, that the Yorks were making a bid for power. It was denied but then such things were always denied. I knew though that every rumour had a tiny spark of truth in it somewhere.

Margaret had a trouble-free pregnancy, despite the gloom-mongers among her ladies who tried to stop her doing this and that, tried to make her rest, not to ride or walk or dance. She would shut them up by referring to me as a prime example of how to carry a child, have an easy birth and carry on life. My brood of children and my ease of giving birth were enough to stop their silly talk. Margaret did all she wanted to do and in the end her child arrived without any of the problems they foretold for her. Just as I knew it would. I got some strange looks and I knew they talked about me behind my back, but what was unusual about that? We all lived with that kind of activity from the moment we set an embroidered slipper inside the court. What they really thought of me and what I really thought of them is something I need to keep to myself at all times. Even now.

Edward, son and heir to Henry VI, arrived in October 1453, much to the intense pleasure of his mother and the court. He was a healthy child from the start, which was pleasing. Margaret went to live in Grenewich to rest and to take care of her son and half the court went with her. Henry was taken care of by his physicians who in truth could do little for him but hope he found his own way out of the dark cloud he was under. No one really understood his condition and could not help him because of that.

More rumours began, people saying that Henry was not the father of the new Prince of Wales, a story we dismissed as so much rubbish. Unfortunately they persisted, some even going so far as to name possible names. The sad fact was, Henry was regarded as a monk more than a king and a monkish devout person could not father a child, they said. They were wrong. Edward looked exactly like his father and had his mother's personality. Anyone who knew them both would have no doubts of the child's paternity. Anyone who really knew Margaret of Anjou would know the talk was nonsensical. She was no more likely to take a lover than I was and that was a certainty.

Although life seemed good, things were troubling me; I could sense problems looming in all directions without knowing clearly where they were coming from. My usual intuitions were failing me, perhaps because I was too close to everything. When I could, I left court and returned home. Time spent away from that hothouse of rumour and innuendo, of power struggles and sheer backbiting nastiness at times would be good anyway, I thought. I was worried about Margaret's anti-York campaign, her attempts to sideline the duke and then attempt to have him assassinated. That was sure to bring trouble down on the court in some way or another. The duke would not stand for that kind of treatment, even from the Queen of England. It was obvious to anyone who knew her well that advice such as 'why not moderate your attitude to York?' would be rejected out of hand and the person might lose their position with her. It was not worth losing your place in court over it. I thought, if she was foolish enough not to see what she was doing, that was her problem and not anyone else's.

The facts were, the queen was not popular and so it was easy to see where conflict might arise. With her actions and her personality ... At times she had a bitter tongue and was fiercely possessive of her son, her position and the future of her family. All of this was the same ambition I had, but without her unpopularity – at that time – and I did not want to become too embroiled in the problems for fear of them reflecting on the Wydvilles.

When I returned to Grafton, I hastened to see Clary, to discuss with her things I was bothered about, some of my visions, predictions and scenes seen in the scrying bowl. I found her ill in bed with fever, which worried me but I had to talk to her. She wrapped a cloth over her mouth and nose, so as not to breathe on me.

"My lady, it is good to see you." The words were muffled through the cloth but I heard them just the same.

"I am sorry to find you ill. Is there anything I can do for you?"

"No, thank you. I have been waiting for you to come; you have many questions, many things have happened since you were in that place – in London. Please, sit."

I had hardly sat down on the stool when she went into her trance state. The guardian spoke only briefly with me, no doubt to conserve her strength.

"My lady, you fear for many things. Some will come to pass. There is conflict ahead. Be warned, be prepared. Your visions are true. Trust in yourself. You have been a good student. We are pleased with you."

And that was it. Nothing to settle my worried mind but at least I knew that what I had seen was right. In many ways that was enough. We cannot all have perfect answers to our questions, life isn't like that.

Clary coughed and spluttered when she came out of her trance and I got fresh water for her to drink. "I won't bother you now," I told her. "I'll return home and send my physician to you."

She waved a dismissive hand. "Please, do not trouble yourself. I will be all right."

"I have to. I-"

She looked at me with red rimmed, dulled eyes. The fever was burning her up.

"Because I care about you," I said eventually.

That produced a smile, albeit a small one. "Thank you. I waited; I needed to wait to give you your answers. You have been good to me. Go now, before this illness reaches you."

I was reluctant to leave, desperately wanting to arrange something for her to eat, to make some medicine to make her better but then I reasoned she probably did not want to eat and she had her own potions. It was more than that, though. I had the strongest feeling I would not see her again and that hurt deeply, more than I thought it would. She had shown me a different world, one I could use to enhance my life. I hated the thought of leaving her, of losing her. I did not want to walk away and leave her on her own. I had no choice. If I stayed I risked catching whatever it was she had and that would never do.

With a smile I hoped was encouraging, I again gave her my thanks, tucked a coin into her hand and left.

Outside, the air was fresh and cool, unlike the heated atmosphere in the little cottage. I rode back home wondering if the words of the guardian had indicated what I had sensed as I left. 'You have been a good student.' Not 'you are a good student' for I felt there was still more she could teach me.

Although I feared her life was ending and thought there was little anyone could do, I had to follow through with the promise and asked my physician to visit. He went straight to her but my fears were confirmed when he returned to tell me she was beyond help and that he felt her time was short.

I had the message that she had died just two days later. One of the villagers came with the news. She had no family, they said, so I arranged for her burial and paid for everything. It was a very small 'thank you' for all I had received in the way of friendship, help and guidance over several years. I mourned, for without her I was on my own in a world which appeared to be falling apart, with no friend who understood the world beyond the veil as she did. Was that selfish of me, I wondered, reasoning as I did so that she was out of this vale of tears and into the glories of the other side. I realised then I was grieving for my loss, not hers.

At least, I thought I was on my own until the day of the funeral. I went, against all convention and society mores; I went and stood by her grave which had been dug in the corner of the churchyard. It was overhung with trees which she loved, they would drop their concealing covering leaves on her every Autumn. As the simple coffin was lowered into the ground, I became aware of the scent of flowers and looked round. There were no flowers. There were scant few mourners, villagers who had no doubt consulted her and myself and I carried no flowers. In that moment I knew I was not alone and would not be, either. I had the people from the other side of the veil with me, probably even Clary herself, even if she was no longer here. I wondered how long it would be before I heard her name called in the breeze or in the sound of a child's voice singing a ditty. Not long, I thought, and took comfort from that.

71

Being alone, in the accepted sense of the word, meant I had to rely completely on my own interpretation of visions and dreams, signs and portents. I found that I was able to see more clearly and wondered if Clary was helping me from beyond the veil. The scrying bowl gave up its secrets more readily, no black swirls now, just clarity of vision. It did not escape me that clarity and Clary were very similar words.

In the bowl I saw conflict. Great armies attacked one another and men were killed. Castles were toppled, indicating dynasties falling. I felt fear churning in the pit of my stomach when I saw it and prayed endlessly that my beloved Richard would be protected. I could not imagine life without him.

I looked for his coming by the hour, even when he was busy with the king's affairs, fighting in France, or helping put down some insurrection in this country led by someone called Jack Cade. I did not bother my head with the whys and wherefores of all that, I had too much else to think about. My daughter Elizabeth was not producing the heirs her husband needed, I had to look into that. I was carrying again, the result of Richard returning triumphant from France, I do believe, and being made Seneschal of Aquitaine to head an expedition which failed to take off. Politics again. At least that meant he stayed home for a short while, even if he was impatient and frustrated and often downright angry at the constant delays which finally ended the whole thing.

My children were growing fast and becoming all that I wanted them to be. John in particular would make a fine soldier, I thought. I had not yet seen the 'adventurer' son the guide had spoken of, but I had learned that what they said would happen did not always mean tomorrow or the week ahead, it sometimes meant years ahead. It was obvious they could see much further than us and in doing so, often forgot that we were only human and could not see that far into the future.

My daughter Margaret arrived in 1453. She was named for the Queen and the Queen honoured me by being her godmother. It was enough to keep me busy whilst Richard was away in Calais, attending to the king's business, getting home whenever he could which was never often enough for me, but then I always was possessive of the time I spent with my beloved husband. He had matured into the most handsome man in the world, let alone England. Greying hair suited him, marks of experience carved his face and made it more loved by me. His strength had not failed; he was as virile and fit as ever, hardly ever getting as much as a cold. He viewed the regency of the duke of York with great concern and spoke of it with an intensity that was unusual for him. He asked if had seen anything in my scrying, which he had learned to depend on and I had to confess I had seen conflict and even admitted, in a rare moment of honesty, that I had seen the Lancastrian arms break and dissolve. I did not say I had seen it some years before and had held the secret all this time, he would not have understood my keeping that to myself. But in truth, who would have thought it? The Lancastrian king seemed firmly set on the throne, who could have foreseen the disaster of his breakdown which allowed a York to take over?

Those who see further than I, that's who. I should have taken more notice of that vision when it happened.

We talked about it and he looked even more serious and worried than he had before. "We have to think on this," he told me. "It could mean more conflict." Oh yes, that had been there, so much of it. I knew our lives would be tainted by the battle fever and blood of the dead before too long. I was frankly terrified for the health and well being of my men but knew there was nothing I could do about it. In many ways that made it worse. Most things are under our control, we can organise, direct, confront or run away, whichever is right for the situation. When it comes to the monarchy and their demands … there is no such solution. You had to wait it out and go with what they want or risk losing everything. The trouble was, if I lost my husband I would quite simply have lost everything anyway.

It was almost a year to the day when the king regained his senses and took control of his government again. He immediately began making concessions to the Yorks, even talking of appointing the duke of York as heir to the throne. It caused uproar.

I stayed out of it. I was Lancastrian by marriage and affiliation, I did not want the Yorks interfering with the future plans for my family but I had in mind the vision of conflict breaking out and men being killed. I feared anew for my family, my husband, my sons. The sick feeling came back in force and stayed, upsetting me considerably. I could hardly eat or drink for the terrible feeling I had.

My sons: Richard arrived next, long-limbed, dark haired, demanding from the start and then Edward, who I quickly realised would be the adventurer I had been told of, for no nursemaid could keep track of him. He was set on exploring the moment he found his baby feet and could escape their supervision.

Life. Difficult, complicated politics, Yorkists set against Lancastrians, family problems, a daughter married for some years without producing a child, in London, a queen seemingly making herself more unpopular by the day and I still her favourite, in Grafton, my seer, wise woman and friend departed this life to the other side – I missed her still – a husband spending too much time in Calais and not enough at home and overall, the inevitability of the conflict I saw over and over again.

There were nights I simply cried and cried, with no one to console me, not even those who were hovering just outside my line of sight. They tried, but they were not human, they were not Richard Wydeville, the only one my arms longed for.

Chapter Seven

For those who are interested in such details, I bore two more children before I stopped being capable of doing it, Thomas and then Agnes. She did not live very long. Now you know. That is all of my children. I was a fertile wife and devoted mother, as best as I could be, with the demands of court, of the house and of life generally. They knew to obey me, if nothing else! I demanded obedience and got it, because that was the training they needed for their future. I gave them love and they knew it. Whether I had their love in return is something I never really knew. I could not know how they viewed me, a distant mother, perhaps, ever leaving them to go to London or organising their lives when back in Grafton. I had no way of knowing if they resented their lessons, their training, their attendance at services or – it has just occurred to me – even if they liked their tutors, nursemaids and others. It never crossed my mind to ask if they were happy or unhappy with what they had. I gave it, they took it. End of discussion, as it were. Did they rely on each other for companionship? I did not know. I took little to no part in their actual upbringing, that was what nursemaids and tutors were for, after all. What I saw each time I returned to Grafton was attractive girls and handsome boys, well dressed, well behaved with impeccable manners and a high level of education. That is what I had arranged, that is what I got. But likes and loves … I never asked. It has just occurred to me perhaps I should have done.

Am I justifying myself here? Maybe I am but I had of necessity to leave them alone more than I would have liked, alone that is, with their great army of servants, tutors, nursemaids, riding instructors, arms instructors, seamstresses and tailors, cooks and laundry women, taking care of every aspect of their lives. I did all I could and then left them to go to London where their future was in the hands of others, people I had to flatter, cajole and be constantly on good terms with, regardless of how I felt about them, to ensure our continual wealth and fortune. That's how I saw it, anyway.

It seemed 'forces' were at work behind the scenes. Margaret spoke to me in secret of the 'evil' she felt was being done by Richard duke of York who, she declared, was undermining her position with the king. I tried to dissuade her but against all sensible advice, she called a great council - and excluded the Yorks.

And so the grounds were laid for the first of the conflicts I had seen. There was no way the Yorks would stand for that and they began their bid for power immediately. In 1455 my beloved Richard rode out to fight for the Lancastrian cause against the Yorks at a place called St Albans.

I spent the entire time in seclusion in my room, eating nothing, drinking nothing, ignoring all calls for my attention, staring into my scrying bowl, watching for any vision that would tell me if my man lived or died. I saw a repeat of the battles I had seen before, man for man, blow for blow, I could anticipate who would fall down next, for I had seen them several times.

What the bowl did not tell me was who were the victors and who the men were who died. That was why my heart was in my mouth and I could not eat or drink or speak until it was over, until Richard rode home again. The household knew of my feelings, I had made it perfectly clear to them I was to be left alone and God protect anyone who disobeyed me, no matter what. It had to be a life and death situation involving one of my children before I would leave my room at someone's summons.

I heard that it was a Yorkist victory. Messengers arrived in advance of my husband to tell us that the duke of York had captured the king and the Earl of Warwick kept him as prisoner, but Margaret had escaped. God forgive me, for a moment I thought how bad a thing that was, having come to the reluctant conclusion that Margaret of Anjou would never rest until the York claims to the throne were crushed and the duke of York was out of her life. I recalled the moment I saw the blood dripping through and from her hands at her coronation, a truly frightening moment, one that for a brief heartbeat had made me wish I did not have the ability to see such things. I recalled it at that moment, then I controlled the thought, sent it back where it came from, into the box marked 'female flutters' and nailed down the lid. Such thoughts could not be permitted space and time. I had a job to do. I did it with every tool I had and if that included the ability to see into the future, then I would use that too. I could not let my aversion to anything I saw put me off using the still, talent, gift, call it what you will. It was there, I used it.

Richard rode home with his men, all of whom had survived, I am pleased to say, if bruised, battered, exhausted and disheartened. I didn't want details; I wanted my man safe and well. I thanked God most fervently for his safety as soon as I had him back in my arms and his bed to rest. I nursed him and fussed over him and said 'ignore it' but of course he couldn't. To lose a battle is always crushing, all those Lancastrian supporters dying in vain. Personally I thought all the men who died had done so in vain but I dared not say it to a fighting man.

Everything quietened for a while, but only on the surface. There were currents of discontent, of outright anger, of savage words and arguments that boded ill for the future. There were more battles to come, that was both obvious and a fact of life. I could not escape that, any more than I could escape the confines of court and live in peace in Grafton.

But there were times I wished Margaret of Anjou to the furthest corners of the world so that peace would return and I could be sure of my future with the man I loved so much. There was an additional fear. As my sons grew older, they too would be involved in battles. It scared me more than I can say. I could do just so much with prayers and pleas for protection. No matter what we did, any of us, the time of death for each person is in God's hands and we have to live with the consequences of that. It didn't stop me worrying.

To offset the darkness and gloom I was feeling, I received a letter telling me that Elizabeth was carrying. At last, I thought! What took her so long? She was young, healthy and capable, surely! I hoped for a flock of grandchildren to match my children, so the Wydeville name would spread across England. Dreams, I had many of them. That was just one.

After a trouble free pregnancy, she gave birth to Thomas in 1457. It helped me stop worrying for a while, but then news broke that an associate of Margaret's, a French general, had raised an army of 4000 men from Honfleur, sailed across the Channel, landed on English soil and burned Sandwich to the ground.

England went mad; those of us who knew about it were appalled. The populace as a whole were mostly concerned with their own lives but village elders and town mayors and the like were all up in arms about it, demanding protection from the French. Margaret's name became bandied about in crude jokes and songs. She tried to hide from the public but a Queen cannot hide, her actions rebound on her all the time. More and more I was glad I married a 'mere' knight, that I did not aspire to Queenship. But having said that … I feel I would have made a better Queen than she did. Ah, do I not cast aside the favouritism and the favours and the friendship and the benefits I received from being there in saying such a thing? But it is the truth. Anyone associated with a Queen who does something stupid, outrageous, whatever, brings down calumny on the head of the Queen and her court. So it was with this invasion, for it was nothing short of that. She suffered for something her kinsman had instigated. There were deaths; it was a disaster, both politically and locally. She had the ability to create enemies, bitter enemies at that, who then attacked her and tried to dislodge her husband from the throne. I admired her for fighting on alone, he still being a prisoner of Warwick, but I felt she was doing it all the wrong way. The more she argued and fought back, the more determined the Yorkists were to overcome and claim what they said was rightfully theirs – the throne of England.

The whole mess that was the Honfleur invasion had another effect which I did not foresee, even with all my abilities. The Earl of Warwick was given the task of keeping the sea safe for at least three years. He was already Captain of Calais so this added to his standing. Margaret hated the Earl of Warwick... this was to have consequences for the Wydevilles which were quite unexpected. When it happened, it annoyed me considerably, for it should not have been unexpected. Unless I had ignored, misheard or simply not seen the message when it was given to me, I should have known. Ah, the key is - if it was given to me. We are not told everything, unfortunately. Would that we were! But that was for the future. Before then, I had the good news that Elizabeth had become pregnant again. She gave birth to her second son, Richard, in 1458. I was well pleased. She had two handsome, healthy sons and both she and her husband were rightly very proud of them.

It would be good at this point if I could say life was peaceful but there were ripples of discontent all over the place, ripples? More like big waves. What had been under the surface for some time had begun to show in small outbreaks of violence, a good deal of shouting and a lot of hot air from a lot of men who should have known better. We heard rumours and stories and more rumours, some of which we discounted, some of which we mulled over and some of which we took seriously from the start.

In all this confusion and pending violence, the duke of York became worried about his family and sent Lady Cecily and their two young sons to Ludlow for protection. Fotheringhay was obviously not secure enough for them. That was worrying in itself. He must have been anticipating an attack there, but unfortunately he miscalculated, the attack came at Ludlow itself. Battles were going on here and there around Ludlow, with victory for this side and the other, nothing decisive, but the Blore Heath fiasco, I can call it nothing less, began the serious slide into all out conflict between the two major forces. The Yorkists were out numbered and out manoeuvred too, they were virtually cut to pieces on the battlefield.

This is what I heard; this is what was conveyed to us in our home at Grafton. How much was exaggerated, how much was understated, I have no way of knowing. I tell you what I know and no more. I heard a tale that Margaret watched the battle from a nearby vantage point. It was a tale, no more than that. I know she was securely in London at that time, marshalling her forces, directing her commanders, being the Queen she always was, directing everything from her position at the top. Where such stories come from I have no idea. Maybe from her detractors, who liked to depict her as bloodthirsty and savage and delighting in seeing men die? Who knows why these stories begin? Or who thinks of them in the first place?

With the Lancastrian army on the move it was inevitable, to my way of thinking anyway, that they would eventually sack Ludlow Castle and steal its treasures.

Here comes the setting up of one of our future problems: the duke of York and his second son escaped to Ireland, Edward of March and Lord Salisbury went to Calais. We heard tell that Lady Cecily and her two youngest sons, George and Richard, were taken prisoner and carted off somewhere for safety. Lucky woman, she was better out of it but oh the heartbreak of having your husband and sons in different places with different problems – the central one being simply that she was without them. I knew that feeling well.

You are no doubt wondering how this set up problems for us in the future. It went like this ... there were three earls in Calais, scheming and planning and manipulating and generally getting under the Queen's skin one way and another. Richard was commissioned to raise a fleet to go there and sort them out once and for all. We had to go to Sandwich to supervise all this.

We. Richard decided to take Antony with him and I said I would go too, as it was coming up to the Christmas period and I did not want to spend another Christmas without my husband. We argued but I won. More fool me; I should have listened to my instincts. But then again, the bowl was silent on this particular episode.

It was bitterly cold when we went, wrapped from head to foot in furs, plodding through the bleak winter countryside, counting our blessings, such as they were, we were together, we were reasonably warm, we had an armed guard (our own men whom we trusted) and a warm Inn to stay in when we got there. I hoped. No one grumbled for a change, not in my hearing anyway and we finally rode into the newly rebuilt town. I wondered about that, it looked as if it had been there forever, but I knew it had been burned down. Surprising how quickly timber buildings aged when close to the influence of the sea.

That aside, we had a comfortable Inn, we celebrated Christmas and I was content and happy to be with the two men in my life. Richard was busy with plans for the fleet, messengers coming and going all the time. What we did not realise and stupidly, we should have done – maybe I should have packed my scrying bowl into my luggage but didn't – our every move was being reported to the earls in Calais who were busy making their own plans, as we discovered to our cost.

One cold January night – and believe me it was cold, even under thick furs I was shivering – there was someone hammering on the door. After what seemed like an age, the Landlord opened it and what sounded like a group of armed men literally charged in. I heard all this, heard him open the door, heard his quavering 'what do you-" heard the booted feet on the stairs and knew, somehow just knew, they were coming for us.

They were.

"You're coming with us!" No argument. No chance to fight. Too many of them and we were at a disadvantage anyway, they being fully dressed and armed and we being in bed and having weapons by our side but not in our hands. We were allowed to dress, grab our thickest furs and a few possessions before we were hustled down the stairs, four men to each of us, pushed out into the cold night, down the quay, on a gangplank and onto a stinking ship. We had to cross the turbulent waters and then, what seemed like days later but was no doubt only hours, landed at what we were told was Calais. The journey had seemed endless. I was torn between terror and anger in alternate bursts of emotion. I wanted to cry but dared not, for fear of someone seeing and pointing a finger.

83

There were men with torches on the quayside, no doubt delegated to light our way off the ship, but after that we were left to stumble along in the dark with those who had captured us. I use the word advisedly. No one spoke, not even a curse or an insult. I found that strange, maybe they had been ordered to be quiet.

And then we were there, in an elaborate building, pushed through corridors and into a room heated by a huge fire, not that we were allowed to get near it, mind, and there they were, the hated Yorkists. At that time they were hated, anyway. Remember we were Lancastrians to our very bones then. Warwick was grinning with what I can only describe as a malicious look, Edward of March was doing his best to look older than his years and Salisbury looked bored.

We were told that we had been 'arrested' by the Yorkists, that our attempts to put a fleet together were pathetic and that although I would be released – nice of them, I thought – my husband and son would remain prisoners until they saw fit to release them. I caught Antony's look of abject terror. Poor boy, he had not been away from home once in his life and here he was, a prisoner of the Yorkist faction in another country. I tried to smile with some confidence but my terror was for a different reason, I was about to leave my beloved husband in someone else's hands. Someone I did not trust. Three 'someone's' I did not trust, in truth. None of us spoke a word in return.

I was allowed to stay with Richard and Antony overnight. We were put into a side room, without heat, with one small lantern and nothing else. During the long night hours I tried to talk to my son and instil in him the fact I would be working for his release from the moment I set foot in England again and I told Richard, my love and my life, that I would not forget him for a moment. Somehow we slept briefly and then the dawn came. Men slammed open the door and grabbed my arm. I was hustled away without so much as a scrap of bread or something to drink and pushed back on the ship which sailed for England on the tide almost immediately.

If I thought the journey going over to Calais was long, the one going back lasted an eternity. I was treated with courtesy, even given food and drink but it almost choked me. I wanted my husband, my son and my life back.

It was some months before they were returned to me.

Chapter Eight

There were times when I wished I had not 'seen' what was to come, conflict after conflict, but I realised and accepted that those who walk that path have to accept the responsibility that comes with walking it. You cannot stop the gift, if it can be called that, and start it again when it suits you. What you see, you see - and accept. I had seen battles and battles were fought all over the place.

England's two main factions seemed determined to tear each other apart without regard for the suffering it caused.

The battle of Wakefield, fought during the Twelve Days of Christmas, ended with the death of the duke of York, the Earl of Salisbury and the duke's second son, Edmund, Earl of Rutland, said to have been murdered in cold blood on the battlefield. Margaret showed her vicious vindictive nature that time by ordering their severed heads be displayed on the spikes at Micklegate, the entrance to the city of York. I thought it an action she could well have avoided; she should have been magnanimous in her victory. I searched my own heart and knew that, despite my ability to over react at times, I would not have ordered that, simply because it is the quickest way to make a mortal enemy of your opponent, one that will never be placated until the dying is finally done. I wept in the secrecy of my room for Lady Cecily and the sons who lived on, for they had to bear the legacy of that terrible action.

In the February an array went out for yet another battle at St Albans and this time Antony was called too. In the name of Heaven, how could any mother stand that, her husband and son going off to battle together, her son going for the first time?

I had no choice. They were bound by oath to answer an array and so they went, Antony proud and almost jubilant at going into battle, for all he knew of the perils of fighting men who were battle experienced and hardened where he was not. I had to rely on the extensive training he had undergone to see him through. I spent the day, as before, in solitude, no drink, no food, no talking. It always seemed wrong to act 'normal' whilst my men were fighting for their lives and their king, on some battlefield that would no doubt be forgotten in a hundred years' time.

The day could have been worse, but not by much. My husband and son came back, Elizabeth's husband did not. It was a great Lancastrian victory but that did not ease the pain of a daughter who was suddenly a widow, with two small sons and, as it transpired, no home after legal action was taken. We took her back in the Bury, of course. I adored the boys and was glad to have them there but her heartache was sad to see.

With a Lancastrian victory the king was released from captivity and restored to his wife. I wondered how Margaret felt having to defer to her husband again and I wondered how he felt, for I believed she had become harder, more determined, more difficult than she had been before. Her feelings showed in her speech and her decisions, revealing most of all her hatred of all things Yorkist. I had no chance to find out how she felt from her words to me; she was busy with her scheming and battle plans generally and did not want to talk very much to her ladies. I did think, by design, the King was being left out of the picture. Then again, I wondered how much he would understand what was going on. The rumours which were flying around at that time said he had slipped into dementia, for he had been seen laughing and singing whilst the St Albans battle had been going on. I feared the poor man was beyond help. I spent as much time at home as I could without offending the Queen. I blamed illness among the children, the needs of the home, all manner of legitimate reasons not to be

87

with her. Foolishly I found myself constantly watching her hands to see if blood dripped from them. It never did. It would have been too much for me if it had. I think I would have renounced the pathway there and then!

There was no peace. Strife continued, argument continued and it seemed like no time at all before my men, as I now thought of them, were called to arms again. Another battle loomed, this one at Towton.

Elizabeth and I attended services on Palm Sunday, every one of them. It was on that day the two armies were to meet and we were both consumed with worry over our men who were going out there, fighting for their lives as well as fighting for the Lancastrian cause. We waited all day, neither of us eating, drinking or speaking. This was not something I had asked Elizabeth to do, she just did not want to do any of those things. In that way she was so like me. She had dark shadows under her eyes as she relived the waiting for the end of the St Albans battle when, instead of John Grey, a messenger had come with the news he had been struck down. She had loved her husband and still grieved endlessly for him. I don't know, for no one said, if I carried the same dark shadows but I knew the ache of not knowing, of waiting on every footfall, every hoof-beat that might be a messenger bringing us the bad news we did not want to hear. It was a nightmare of waiting, every moment stretched to many times its length, the day passing as slowly as a year. We did not speak for what could we say?

We had a long wearying wait. It was not until dawn broke the next morning that Richard and Antony walked in, leading lathered exhausted foam flecked horses and looking about fit to drop in their tracks themselves. Their squires looked equally weary. A group of men at arms followed them, exhaustion showing in every line of their bodies. No orders were necessary, stable hands took the horses and led them gently, step by step, into the stables. The men dispersed to their quarters as I held Richard tight for a moment and then took him to our room, knowing that the Seneschal had Antony in his grasp. We asked no questions, just looked for wounds and found none. We got them into their beds and they slept for the rest of the day. I sat by the bed holding Richard's hand, all but in tears again. I did so hate battles, but what woman didn't? We sit at home, we watch them ride out in their armour, their horses gleaming from all the grooming, their arms glittering in the sun - if there is any - not knowing if we will see them alive again. They could well be brought home on a shield or a litter, battered, broken, dead. They could come home wounded to the point of death; they could come home wounded and take months to heal. Or, like my two, come home pummelled and battered and bruised and exhausted with the battle fever gone from their eyes and nothing but terror combined with relief that it was done and they still lived.

I realised, as I sat there, I had not even found out who won the battle. It didn't matter at that moment, relief was everything, relief that they were alive and not wounded, even if damaged in their minds for a while. I had never seen Richard in such an exhausted state; it must have been a very long and very vicious battle indeed.

I learned more when he finally woke, seeking food, ale and consolation.

"We lost," were his next words. "Jacquetta, it was-" Tears began pouring down his face. I had never seen Richard cry, it cut me to the very heart. I held him tight and told him he was safe now and not to worry.

"It was hell," he said after a while. "Snow in our faces, arrows flying through the snow, men trampled, they didn't die from fighting, they died from being trampled into the mud. It went on and on and on … I saw Edward of March, like some ancient god he was, riding a blood splattered destrier, armour covered in blood, shouting, raging, encouraging and his men rallied and followed him and we were crushed." He stopped for a moment, looking at nothing. Then he shuddered, reached for the ale, drank half the cup and then looked at me.

"All I could see was your face, love of my life. I was so afraid I would not come back to you."

"But you did, you're here, you're safe."

"Until the next time. There is always a next time, isn't there?"

"Yes." I shuddered and vowed not to look into the scrying bowl for at least a week. It was not something I could give up, though; I needed to know what was going to happen. I needed the knowledge to gather strength for what was to come.

"We were captured, we were prisoners for a short time but the Yorkists were letting everyone go. I suppose they had made their point with their victory. Oh the dead, there were so many dead!"

"Hush, rest, let it go."

"When I'm rested, we need to talk." He caught my hand and held it so tight it almost hurt. "We need to decide which side we're on. I believe the Lancastrian cause is over."

"Hush. It's enough for now. There is time. Now I need to see how Antony is. You were both exhausted when you got back."

"Have you not seen Antony yet? Go to him! Let me tell you, he was magnificent. God knows I am so proud of our son! Only his second battle and he fought like a man possessed! I don't know how many he

90

accounted for but he was truly a fighting man. He was as scared as me before we started but then it was as if he was not afraid of anything or anyone!"

"I'll let him know you're proud of him. Now, rest!"

Knowing Richard was all right, talking coherently and with no visible wounds, I went to Antony's room which was shaded from the morning light by shutters.

My son was lying in his bed, quiet, almost subdued. He had a bad bruise on his forehead and darkly shadowed eyes. If he had other bruises, I didn't see them. I anticipated that he did, you cannot fight for hours with men determined to kill you, no matter what, without being hurt physically and mentally.

"Mother." He just about managed to look up when I went in. His voice betrayed his utter exhaustion.

"Antony. How do you feel?" I sat on the chair by his bed and reached for his hand. It felt cold and almost lifeless.

"Weary." He lifted the other arm and let it drop again. "As if I'll never be able to use my limbs properly again."

"You'll be all right but it'll take a while. Your father tells me he is incredibly proud of you, the way you fought, the way you acquitted yourself in battle."

"Thank you." Some of the darkness lifted from his eyes at that. "It was hell, Mother, it really was. I never realised…I thought St Albans was bad but this one…"

"Few do, unless they are in the middle of it. Do you hurt?"

"I hurt everywhere." He grinned and it lifted the mood for a moment. "Bruises everywhere, it seems, but no gashes, no blood loss. Oh, but I'm tired!"

"Food and drink, my beloved son, then go back to sleep. You did well, no one could have asked more of you."

His mood changed in that instant. "I wish we had won," he said in what was virtually a whisper.

"Your father is proud of you, win or lose." I got up and began to walk to the door. "I'll arrange for food brought up to you. Stay there. Your father says we'll talk about it all when you both recover."

"How are the horses?" he asked as I stood with my hand on the latch of the door.

"I don't know. I'll send someone to find out and let you know. It was good of you both to walk them home, rather than ride to the very last."

"We would have killed them if we had. They were worn out, poor beasts."

"Rest!" I ordered and left his room, hurrying downstairs, trying to hide my tears. In the middle of his physical and mental pain, he thought of the horses. My son had a great heart and I welcomed that. It would make him a compassionate man.

It was a full night and a day before either of them emerged from their beds and even then they looked weary. Holding a cup or a knife seemed to be an effort. Fighting all those hours with battle-axes and swords had strained their muscles to the limit. The horses, I could tell them, were fine, having been fed well, rested and groomed. Richard told me they had walked the final two miles, knowing that the animals were on the point of dropping by then. The squires and men, those who had survived the battle, were still resting. We left them to rest; we could ask no more of them. We would mourn the ones who had been lost when we had a tally of their names for the record book.

We sat round the fire together, huddled in furs and wraps against the chill, for despite it being just after Palm Sunday, the weather remained bitterly cold. We talked about our future loyalties. Richard insisted that the Lancastrian cause was done, that we had to transfer our allegiance to the Yorks if we were to survive. This went against all our upbringing, of course, and seemed an insult to the memory of the men who had died fighting for the Lancastrian king, but it was clearly the only way forward. I wanted to go and consult those who were with me, but that was not the moment to do it.

Finally I said, "well, there is little we can do right now. We need to let the battle memories fade a little and then, when we get a chance, appeal to Edward of March's good nature and see what happens. At the very least we need a pardon."

"Edward of March?" Richard looked at me in surprise. "Get used to calling him King Edward, my beloved wife. He will have assumed power by now, for sure."

I had not thought of it but of course he was right. Having won such a decisive battle, Edward would be bound to take over. Could England have two living kings?

And, could I go to London and see Margaret and expect her to feel the same toward me? Stupid thought. She would not be there; she would be in exile somewhere with her husband, the one time king. I could go to London and show my face at the court of King Edward IV and see how I was accepted.

What a thought. We had as our king a man about as old as my son Antony but more battle scarred and experienced than he. I wondered what sort of a man Edward was, whether he would be generous in his favours to those who were once Lancastrian, would he look favourably on the Wydevilles … I had to go to find out. I vowed I would go once my two beloved men were fully recovered, just to find out. I had enough contacts in court to be able to go there, regardless of which king we had on the throne. To be honest, and there is no reason for me to be otherwise, is there? I cared not which king was on the throne, provided they looked favourably on the Wydevilles. I could accept Edward of March in place of Henry VI if I had to. King Edward sounded as good to me as King Henry. I recalled that Edward of March was very good-looking, tall and well built and would be the sort of king people would admire. Poor Henry never did have it in him to be regal. I had so often thought of him as 'poor Henry' it was almost his title.

I wondered if I would see Edward of March – damn it, King Edward's – aura when I went there. I would find it useful for my future negotiations if I had some idea of the hidden person, not the public face. I would ask if it could be granted to me. I would ask many things … and see if they were granted to me.

My decision not to use the scrying bowl for a week came to naught. I sat with it that night and before I even looked into it, I smelled the flowers. I was not alone. I never would be and that brought comfort that cannot be paid for or gained from any living person.

"Clary?" I said it aloud as I was by myself at that moment and heard the sound of delicate laughter. "Clary, thank you for everything. It has fared me well so far. I am going to need some help to make this change, so I will be asking for some guidance."

The smell of flowers grew stronger, as if someone was wearing the actual perfume. I smiled, knowing my request had been granted in advance. I could go to London with confidence, knowing I would find out just what I wanted to know.

The spirit world had heard and agreed.

Chapter Nine

King Edward's coronation was held in June of that year. Legally and officially, whichever way you looked at it, England had two crowned kings at the same time. It was up to lawyers, counsellors and others to work out who was the rightful king or whether one was not entitled to the crown because he had deposed the other, even though the other still lived. It was not something I could think about too much and on that point my scrying and visions gave me no answers. All I knew was that we had a King named Edward, the fourth to carry that name and that he had supreme power – at that time. We went, of course, to see the celebrations and the ceremony. Antony came with us. He knew nothing at that time of my skills as a seer and I wanted to keep it that way.

I found it difficult to suppress my feelings when I first saw King Edward, that giant of a man towering above all his courtiers and companions, for his aura was black shot with red. I told myself he had just fought a successful battle, it was bound to be black and red but I did not believe a word I was saying. The smiling face hid something – not evil, I did not think him evil – but I could not name it. The moment passed and he was once again the benevolent king, dispensing favours, smiles, kisses and handshakes. It was obvious he was a man for the ladies, they fawned over him and he responded with passionate kisses and embraces, sometimes whispering things in their ear that made them blush with pleasure.

His brothers were there but I did not get close enough to attempt to assess them. I hoped to see their auras too but that was pushing my abilities a bit. I also wondered if I really wanted to, Edward's had been enough of a shock. It was actually some time before I could form opinions on the York brothers and when I did, it was not that favourable.

Another coronation. It was getting to be a habit but at least this time I did not see blood dripping from anyone's hands. For that small mercy I was extremely grateful. One monarch with bloodied hands was enough. But there was that aura to worry me still. Black shot with red could mean anything. I hoped it was a freakish thing on the day, not that it augured ill for anyone in my life in the future. Did no one else matter? No, not really. I lived and breathed Wydevilles; the rest could go hang as far as I was concerned.

The day was good, the weather held fair, the celebrations were genuine, people seemed really happy to have this charming and handsome king and he in turn seemed pleased to be king, being bashful and almost self-effacing if anyone complimented him on his new fortune. I did not believe it for a moment but it was a good act. I recalled Richard saying he was like some ancient god in battle. I felt Edward of March – I still kept thinking of him that way – could assume any mask that suited him at any given moment, if it furthered his cause.

He saw me at one point and came over as if to speak, but was intercepted by someone and the moment was lost. I was not sorry, I had nothing to say to him that did not sound forced and insincere in the extreme. He would remember well the last time we saw one another. It was not a good memory.

After the coronation we returned to Grafton and picked up the pieces of our lives. I carried on with my schemes for my family. Yes, schemes, I wanted each one to have their birthright, fame, fortune and power. I would do it, no matter what.

I had plans for Antony, whether he realised it or not. One of my friends at court, Lady Scales, had a marriageable widowed daughter, another Elizabeth. She was only a few years older than my son: she would bring him a title, estates, wealth and status. Lady Scales was searching for a husband for her widowed daughter; I was searching for a suitable wife for Antony who already had an illegitimate child. I was not best pleased about the alliance he had formed with this Gwenllian person and the child they produced was a complication I could have done without, but he assured me he did not wish to marry her. Just as well as her family didn't want to marry their daughter into our family. I don't know why, ours was of a much higher standing than theirs, I have to say – so all things considered, it was better that no match was made. He contributed to the upbringing of the child and that was it. I had no contact with her or the family; it was easier that way.

After talks, I would not use the word negotiations in this context, with my friend, a meeting was arranged to see whether the couple liked each other enough to make a dynastic marriage. One golden summer's day, Lady Scales brought her daughter to the Bury to meet Antony. My scrying did not forewarn me of what was to happen – it was love at first sight. I am not sure why I was surprised and shocked, but I was. It was odd, after all, I had married for love and it was surely not beyond the bounds of reason that my children would do so too, but I had not thought of that. I only saw a good marriage to take him several steps up the social ladder toward wealth and fame and standing. Being in love was a bonus and I was glad of it, once I got used to the idea.

It wasn't immediately obvious. The couple walked off together around the grounds, smiling and talking but politely distant from one another. Lady Scales and I sat in my room and talked of families, of court, of everything but the fact her daughter and my son were exploring the possibility of a marriage. They returned after a decent interval and said yes, they were content for the arrangements to be made. We were both delighted and congratulated each other on a fine piece of match making. Only when Elizabeth had gone home with her mother did Antony approach me with a huge smile and open arms.

"You did not tell me I would love her, Mother!"

I was so shocked I do believe I stood with my mouth open for an age whilst he waited for me to speak to him.

"Love?"

"Yes, that feeling you and Father share, you know the one I mean?"

"You've only just met her," I said, staring back at my memories of leaving Rouen Cathedral, seeing the man standing at the head of the guard of honour and knowing I wanted him but not able to mention any of this to my son. That would never do!

"How long does it take?" he asked in return. "I've met her, I love her, she loves me and we can't wait to be married!"

What could I say but congratulations? And keep very quiet about how I came to love his father. Until now, that is. Now the secret is out for all to see and know. Do I care? I do not. I love Richard Wydeville. I loved him then, I love him still. He may be gone from this life but that makes no difference to the way I feel about him.

Even as I looked at Antony I saw, as if overlaid on his smiling face, the broken grief-stricken face of an older man. I knew then that Elizabeth would not outlive him and wondered if he would manage to cope with the heartbreak. If he loved her the way I loved my husband, it would be very difficult for him. 'God forfend' I prayed silently but even as I did, I knew, as I have said, it was not for us to say when anyone died. I prayed instead that he would have years of happiness with her before it happened.

Then the image went and he was back to his young, handsome, smiling self again.

"Thank you, Mother," he said, kissing me and going off to the stables. "Going riding!" he called back. I waved and went into my room. I had much to think about.

The wedding was arranged in Norfolk, that far off area that few visited and even less returned from but it was where the Scales' family lived and so we dutifully trekked across country to Norfolk, to Middleton. It took us several days to get there and we needed a day or two to recover from the journeying. The countryside was so flat you could see for miles and villages and towns seemed so far away I wondered if we would ever reach our destination.

Middleton Hall was beautiful, though, to make up for the hardship of the journey and it was there we attended a small, exclusive and sumptuous ceremony.

And I watched as my son became Lord Scales. I was so proud it was all I could do to act demure and courteous and friendly, without showing that I was bursting to shout to the people there, 'the first Wydeville child has made it in the world!' It was a charming wedding, that is something I have to say, made all the better by their obvious happiness in being together and the love they so clearly shared. She was an attractive woman, Elizabeth Scales, slender and yet with curves, always calm and seemingly demure but strong willed and very determined. Her hair was dark brown and she wore it in curls clustered around her face. Her dress for the wedding was cloth of silver with black bows and lace, which I admired. She told me she had designed it herself and just gave the drawing, which she had done, to her seamstress to make it for her. There seemed no end to her talents. I was content. It was a good marriage.

The Scales family owned a most elegant home not far from London. It was called Newcelles. Once they were settled in there, I ceased to worry about my firstborn son, concentrating instead on the ones left behind in the Bury. They all needed to be married off somewhere, to the right people to gain the right future. Nothing else would do for the Wydevilles.

I reverted to going to London as often as I could and found that Court was entirely different without Margaret. There was a sense of freedom, which seems an odd thing to say, but it was true. Edward ruled everything but in a different way from Margaret, he cajoled, joked and laughed with everyone. He controlled his temper well, I occasionally saw a flare up of anger in his eyes but he always backed off and met any aggression with a smile, a joke, a bawdy comment if it was a man and was much admired by people for this. He was very much his own man, seemingly allowing himself to go along with what others said but then firmly putting both large feet down and stopping whatever it was in its tracks and doing it his own way.

Whilst he flirted with the women and was hearty and friendly with the men, he kept an eye on everything. This I noticed from the start. There was no way you could fool him; he was too sharp for that. Whilst he might appear to be joking with you, he was in fact studying every word you said and every look you wore. He appeared jovial but, as with the temper, there was a ruthless streak below the smiling face. Physically, as I said, he towered over everyone, a huge strong man with stunning good looks. He would be a good catch for some Princess or other royal; there would be many who would want to be his consort. I was wary of him even though his aura no longer contained the flames of red I had seen before and the black had receded considerably. In fact, the aura was more gold than black but it did not stop me being very careful of the new king.

His brother George, duke of Clarence, was different again. He was a smiling, friendly man who could at times turn petulant if things did not go his way. Again, two faces in one person, he appeared friendly but underneath I felt he was seeking his own life and finding people to use in that life. He had a Fool who was more like a squire and close confidant, someone who went with him everywhere, someone else I had to watch for he too was sharp and sent my senses into spikes.

I was even warier of the king's youngest brother, Richard of Gloucester. That man was dangerous. All my instincts warned me against him. I don't think I spoke to him more than a handful of times during my years in Court but it was enough. His look, his piercing eyes, his very presence shouted 'DANGER' to me. My abilities, such as they were, told me this. I recall vividly the first time I saw him. The words '*For a while they will be fulfilled*' came into my mind as if framed in fire. I thought, if anything happened to my family, it would surely be through that man and no other. I knew I had to warn Antony and anyone else who was at court, tell them to avoid him, to have as little to do with him as possible. And yet, on surface, what was there about him to make me so alarmingly worried? He was personable and polite, not friendly but that was not his character. He did not seem to favour bright colours and many jewels, but his clothes were of the highest quality and the jewels he did wear were chosen with great care to complement the clothes, rather than him wearing them for the sake of ostentatious show. To me he was pure Plantagenet, pure York but there was more to it than that. I could just about cope with that, or could I? I was still having difficulties with the change of affiliation. That was because from the age of 17 I had been Lancastrian through my marriage to poor old John and through my Richard's devoted service to the Lancastrian king. To suddenly decide you are on the other side takes a leap of faith that is sometimes hard to live with. I was still referred to as the dowager Duchess of Bedford, once married to someone who had been a Lancastrian duke. I vowed to pray harder about it, so I could reconcile myself to the changing circumstances in which we found ourselves.

Richard's plea to the new King for pardon had been granted; Earl Rivers was welcome at court and so I could go there openly and carry on the work I had begun. I was able to delight in the fact that Antony had taken his seat in Parliament as Lord Scales of Neucelles, the name coming from that fine family home he and Elizabeth had in Hertfordshire. It was close enough to London for him to be able to carry out Parliamentary duties, attend court and deal with all the many matters which had arisen due to his new status, all without too much travelling. He had a business manager, estate managers and much to occupy his days. I hardly saw him but that was to be expected, with a new wife as well to keep him busy... what was pleasing was the great love I saw between them when they were together. As I said, she was an attractive woman with great style and dignity and he was amazingly handsome. They made a good couple. I was well pleased with that decision.

I kept meaning to ask Antony what his relationship with the king and the king's brothers was like but somehow we never discussed that, it was talk of Elizabeth, of his estates, of his many duties, which occupied our time together. I was waiting anxiously for news of a grandchild but that didn't seem to be happening. I knew Elizabeth Scales was childless from her first marriage and hoped that was not a bad sign. I vowed to go scrying when I returned to the Bury. As soon as possible at that point, as I needed time to absorb all the new impressions, new people, new alliances which I had to think through to see where I stood.

Where was my husband in all this? Trying not to draw too much attention to himself whilst letting people know he was there. It was a game, this life at court, don't be too pushy but don't be too withdrawn, let people know you are there without making it obvious. Watch what you say and whom you say it to ... the 'rules' were endless and it took skilled players to successfully cope with the maze of conspiracy. I had experienced years of it by then and still needed to learn more, now that there were a whole batch of new players in the game, starting with the new king, his two brothers, his many advisors and friends, each of whom had their own ideas about what they wanted in the future. I knew what I wanted; the game plan was to make sure that their ideas matched mine. Then I could have what I wanted, fame and fortune for the Wydevilles.

Back at the Bury I spent time meditating and scrying. I saw no children for Antony and Elizabeth but I did see the two of them together virtually all the time. That was good. I was seeing a true marriage, just as I had, and despite it being childless, that cheered me. I saw darkness around Gloucester, which I guessed from my reaction to him and changing colours around Clarence, which I did not understand. Then the vision cleared and a new one came forward, one which took my breath away. I saw the arms of the Yorks and the Wydevilles come together and become one. What that meant I had no idea but the thought thrilled me through to the point when I became overheated and had to lie down for a while. When my ladies came to see me, I said I had a small moment of dizziness. They put cold cloths on my head and left me alone, which was what I wanted.

I devoted a considerable amount of time to my family after that, assessing them, making plans in my mind which, fortunately, no one knew about. Which one would I give to the church? Every large family has to give one son to the church, at least. I sincerely hoped none of my daughters decided to become a nun, I needed them to make good marriages and continue the line with their offspring. Does this make me sound cold and calculating? My beloved husband was everything I wanted and needed in a man, but he did not have the ambitions I had for our children. I wanted the best, nothing but the best, for all of them. Fame, fortune, no matter how it came, this was my burning desire for them. Well, no matter how it came provided it was respectably gained, that is. Criminality I did not want.

I confess here that my attendance at services was not exactly pious at that time. Instead of devoting my attentions to the Lord God, the Virgin Mary and our Saviour, Jesus Christ, I was watching my sons to see who was showing signs of piety. Now that Antony had left home and was married, successfully in my eyes, I could turn my attention to the others. Antony was extremely pious and for a time I wondered if he would be the one to go into the church. I am glad he did not, he had other things to do in his life.

After a while I decided on Lionel. He seemed to have the right degree of piety, his responses were meant, not gabbled as if he was reciting a piece of literature he had learned or verbs or something like that. He had an ethereal look about him when he took part in the service, so I gently arranged for him to serve at the altar and saw the radiance which he showed at that time. Yes, I had chosen well.

The others were marked down for dynastic marriages, if I could arrange it. I needed a boost, a proper place at court to work at these arrangements. When I was there as Margaret's favourite, I could utilise her influence to get what I sought. Now I was an outsider, the Yorks were in control and it was not the same. And yet that vision of the arms of the Yorks and

Wydevilles coming together was there, ever in my mind. I puzzled endlessly over what it meant and how it would happen. It was one of those things which was kept from me, as if the spirits were playing with me. Perhaps it was best at that time that I did not know. I am not the most patient of people.

For a while life was relatively calm. With Antony spending most of his time either at Neucelles, which I admit was a beautiful home indeed, or in Norfolk or at one or other of their homes, with my other children growing fast and my seeking places for them at court as maids of honour, pages or wherever they could be placed, there was a sense of peace in life that had been missing for a long time. Whatever Margaret was planning, I hoped she kept it to herself, but I knew that her drive for power for herself and for her son would demand she did something sooner or later. I did not know where she was, rumour had it she was in France but she could have been anywhere. I realised I was glad she was not around, surprised that I did not miss for a moment her waspish tongue, her aggression and her virulent drive for power for herself, her husband and her son. She was entirely the wrong wife for a pious meek man who would have been better in a monastery than in court life. No wonder he became ill.

And so things stood in 1464. Elizabeth had accompanied me to London several times but despite being an outstanding beauty, she had failed to attract serious attention of anyone I considered a suitable second husband for her. It looked as if we were going to remain quiet, calm and peaceful for some time.

Until Edward rode into our part of the world and began attending banquets and receptions. Then life changed completely.

Chapter Ten

Do not ask me, at this point, exactly where Elizabeth and Edward met. It was at one of those grand receptions. Being local aristocracy as we were, we had invitations to them all and we went to them all, too. I know she was full of excitement because he had spent much time with her to the exclusion of others, that they had talked long of many things and he seemed smitten. Her words, not mine. I had my doubts and would have had more, had that vision not come back to dance before my eyes. Could it be?

He came often to Northampton, they met often and then came a momentous day, one I hate to recall even now, but I have to say it for it is something no one seems to know about and it explains much.

Elizabeth came to me one day when I was alone in my study, wondering why the bowl had gone dark on me. That was unusual. She knocked and crept in like a little fieldmouse, very unlike my daughter, who usually walked boldly into every room, as I had taught her to do. That was the second unusual thing.

"Mother?" She looked worried and scared at the same time.

"Come in."

"Are you busy?"

"No." I decided on honesty. "I was trying to see into the future but it has gone dark, I can see nothing."

"I didn't know-" She looked scared for a moment.

"You recall my visits to the wise woman?"

"Well, yes, but I thought nothing of them."

"She taught me all I know about divination and scrying. I can usually see something."

Elizabeth looked shocked for a moment. "That's witchcraft, isn't it?"

"No. I don't cast spells, or ill-wish anyone. I use it to see into the future so I can make my plans for the Wydevilles."

"Then I've come at a good moment." She sat down, folding her hands in her lap. "I'm having a baby."

"What!" Stupid, but it was all I could say at that moment. It was hard to breathe, let alone think straight.

"It's Edward's, of course…"

"Well, I would hope it is, as he's the one you've been seeing so much of lately! But-" I ran out of words, shocked beyond belief and yet…

"Well, he says he wants to marry me but we can't claim this child as ours. He needs legitimate heirs." She sounded defiant then, as if I would challenge this statement. I didn't, I was too busy thinking ahead.

"And his proposal is?"

"We get married here, soon, then when the child is born we give it away, then I go to London as his Queen." It all spilled out, as if she had been practising it for some time. She probably had.

There was silence in the room. Outside a bird called, another answered, there was the sound of voices as people came and went, one leading a horse. I could hear the other children out in the grounds somewhere, hear laughter and a high-pitched scream that did not shout danger to me, just childish spirits. I turned away from Elizabeth and looked back into the scrying bowl. She went to speak and I stopped her with a gesture.

I stared into the darkness and watched it swirl and clear, to show me a coming together of the York and Wydeville arms again. Exactly the same as before. It had to be right. But the child … a helpless child, a Wydeville child, to be given away? It was more than I could accept at that moment.

But I had to offset that by the glittering future a marriage such as that would bring the Wydevilles.

107

There was the golden fount of all wealth and power and fame, there was the answer to every prayer I had uttered for my children from the moment Elizabeth had come into the world. It was no coincidence that it was she who would bring about the great change that would accomplish all I had started.

For a second the scene changed to a W with a dagger through it. Then it went and the water reverted to darkness once more. That session was over. It would show me nothing else until the next time I approached it.

Elizabeth had grown impatient as I looked into the bowl. One foot tapped the floor and her hands were not still, as they had been previously. They were restless, trapped birds struggling for freedom.

"I've looked into the future," I told her candidly. "I was shown the arms of the Yorks and Wydevilles coming together and wondered how that would happen. Now you've shown me how it will happen. I just looked into my bowl – which I can assure you only shows me the future, it doesn't show me how to obtain it – and the same vision came." I decided not to tell her about the W, that needed thinking about in private and quiet and calm. This moment was not private, quiet or calm.

"Then you're happy." Her voice was flat, totally devoid of emotion.

"My daughter, first of all, are you happy? Do you want to marry him? Will you be a good wife and consort to such a king, a Yorkist king at that? Remember the Yorks were responsible for your being a widow right now."

She shrugged. "A battle is a battle. It is in God's hands who lives and dies out on the battlefield. As to being happy, I adore Edward. He's everything any woman could want. I don't think for one moment he'll be faithful to me, but as long as I'm his Queen and I bear his heirs, he'll keep me by his side." Then the Wydeville side of her was revealed. "Think what we can do for the family!"

"I already have," I told her and we both smiled. I got up, went over to her and embraced her. "Congratulations! When do you want this wedding?"

"Edward is saying 1st of May here, if that's all right."

"So be it."

"I will be…" she calculated swiftly. "Four months into my term by then. We only have to keep it secret for five months."

"It won't be easy," I mused. "Such an event only comes once in a lifetime to a family."

"But we have to!"

"Of course. I didn't say we wouldn't, I said it wouldn't be easy. There's a difference. We can do it, we'll all know what's at risk if we don't."

It was then she smiled properly, one full of radiant happiness and love and I thought, this might just work out, it just might be all right.

I would have been happier if the cold calculating face of Gloucester had not come into my mind at that moment.

The king was charming and polite when he came to visit the Bury. Nothing was said about the wedding or the child, he just came with his normal retinue on a 'casual' visit, he said, although we rushed around and made sure he had the best of everything whilst he was there. He seemed to have a prodigious capacity for wine; several bottles were consumed before he went away again without so much as a missed step. It was as if he had drunk water the entire time he was with us.

We talked of court, of the people who lived there, of his ambitions to attempt to bring an element of peace to the warring factions, for he knew there were Lancastrian sympathisers even now who would support

Margaret of Anjou if she made a bid for the crown once again on behalf of her poor addled husband, as he described him.

"The Yorks have a clear title to the throne." A statement, not a point for discussion, not a question, even. Edward King of England knew his history and his ancestry well and was determined enough to claim that which he felt was his family's by right. "My father died trying to claim his rightful place as ruler of England. I am doing it for him."

The certainty with which he said this made me see a different Edward again. I had already seen the ruthless one under the jokes and smiles, now I saw the ruler himself, the man who thought he was born to be king. Maybe he was. Had the duke of York lived and claimed the throne, Edward would have been his natural successor. There was a certain 'rightness' about the whole thing which swayed my thinking. In that moment I accepted him as my king – not that he knew otherwise – and husband for my daughter.

Richard accepted him as a fighting man and valiant soldier, as well as a firm and just ruler. He told me that there were many who disagreed with Edward's policies and plans but he could charm his way round them or outright defy them to challenge him. They never did. He was as thrilled with the marriage as I was, the rest of the Wydevilles were quite simply ecstatic, first a wedding and second a royal connection such as we had never dreamed of before.

Elizabeth spoke to me just once of my scrying, telling me she was afraid of it and prayed long that I would bring no evil into our lives because of it. I told her the spirits only came with love but she looked doubtful and worried so we never spoke of it again. Instead we made plans for the 1st May.

We tried our very best. The doorway to the Bury was decorated with flowers for the king's entrance. We set bowls of flowers along the hallway where he would walk. We had what resembled a small altar in the hall and had flowers on that, too. We all had new clothes, I had on a gown of deep green edged and slashed with light green, right pleased I was with it, too. Richard wore lovatt green with russet inserts.

Elizabeth wore an elegant gown of cloth of gold, her glorious hair loose, falling in a cascade of light down her back, held tight to her head with a jewelled net. Her eyes were full of the love light I knew so well and she looked stunningly beautiful. Edward stopped dead in his tracks when he caught sight of her and almost forgot to breathe it seemed, he stood so still and just stared. Then he took control of himself and walked forward, acknowledging us as he did so. He had with him only trusted squires, everyone else had been left wherever they were lodging, he said.

And so, in the relatively humble surroundings of the Wydeville family home, Elizabeth Grey, formerly Wydeville, married Edward of March, King of England.

And I was fit to faint with the pride I felt at the moment of marriage.

Richard was finding it hard to contain the news, this I knew. He smiled all the time; looking as if he wanted to stop the next person he met and tell them his daughter had married the King of England. All that stopped the night he came home from one of the many missions he was still engaged in - different king, same duties – and seemed distracted.

When we finally retired to our room, he said quietly:

"Warwick will be furious when he finds out."

I didn't have to ask 'when Warwick finds out what' for I knew what he meant.

"You've heard something?"

"Just today. He's been arranging a dynastic marriage for Edward with some European princess, or so the talk goes."

'W' with a dagger through it. I shuddered as if a dagger had been thrust into me at that moment. I had promised myself I would think on the vision I saw, but I hadn't, because events had overtaken me and there had been too much else to occupy my thoughts. Now I saw it clearly. Warwick thought he had control of Edward, fool that he was, and called himself Kingmaker. Fool, because no one controlled Edward but Edward himself. He went where he chose, he did what he wanted and he picked his own bride. I knew that, I was surprised Warwick didn't.

"Does this mean trouble?" I asked, not really wanting an answer but needing one so I knew what to do.

"Possibly. I'm not sure yet, beloved one. The problem will come when Edward finally gets round to telling his council what he's done. Then we'll see how Warwick reacts. Right now he thinks he's got it all in hand."

It was worrying. Warwick held a lot of power and had a great deal of influence. Talk had it that Clarence was spending a good deal of time with him, which he excused by saying well, Warwick was his cousin after all. Maybe, but ... people still commented on it. What talk there would have been if everyone had known what we knew – what talk there would be when the truth came out! I almost wanted to wish the time away and be there when the explosion happened, but I had a daughter to protect.

It was difficult to keep her away from court without too many questions being asked. I had to pretend to an illness, a weariness, a small fever, anything to explain why she was not with me. Suddenly I realised

112

people – men – had been looking at her and considering her after all. It had been a close call, any one of them would have been suitable as a husband and we would have lost out on the biggest prize of all. And so I went back to Grafton to take care of her and left them to their speculations of why she was not there and why I was not there, either. That way the 'illness' lie stood up on its feet and none could question it.

It was a long summer. I was concerned for Elizabeth in case anything went wrong. If it did, then the marriage could be announced that much earlier, so part of me said, 'if it is to go wrong, let it…' and another part of me said, 'she is young, healthy and carried her babies to the final day, so…' and this panicking proud worried happy heartbroken mother worried herself so much she lost a lot of weight. Richard said it suited me but I was not happy about it. I did not like having to get my clothes altered to take into account the thinner me. Edward came when he could and talked of ports, shipping, boring things like that with Richard to justify his visit if anyone should ask. Then he spent time with Elizabeth, leaving her both radiant and sad that he had been and he had gone. All the time she grew larger and larger and I kept her indoors, where she walked the hall endlessly for exercise and only occasionally ventured outside, when we were sure there were no visitors. It would not have done for her to be seen.

Nine months to the day she told me she thought she had conceived, a baby boy was born without trouble and the minimum of labour. Elizabeth was ever lucky in that regard. I was there, with only a trusted midwife to do the work. Elizabeth looked on his face once and then turned away, telling me to get him to the wet nurse and to his new home as soon as I could.

For a fleeting moment I thought to hand the child to Antony and his wife but rejected the idea instantly as impractical and cruel. Impractical because Elizabeth had not been seen to be carrying and cruel because the child would be within the family and my daughter would have to see him. He was bathed, baptised and taken to the family we had agreed on. We never saw him again, nor did we hear of him again. That fact has eternally been a pain I carry in my heart.

In compensation, Elizabeth was free to travel to London. This she did as soon as she was able, surrounded by armed guards, riding proud and in style into the capital city of England of which she was Queen, even if no one knew it at the time.

They did shortly after, when the marriage was announced and she was introduced into court as the Queen of England. The uproar could be heard as far as Grafton...

And so the Wydevilles came into prominence and the vision I saw in the bowl was fulfilled. I walked around fit to burst with pride for so long I began to ache in various places, not least my face from smiling all the time.

But ... I have to say this, we all found it very hard at first to do the 'subservient' bit, to remember that the child I once held was now Queen and entitled to deference at all times. Antony fell into the way of it immediately; perhaps our lessons on deference had really sunk home with him. Maybe it was easier, as Elizabeth was older than him, for it to be second nature whereas for Richard and I, this was our daughter, someone who had run to us, been fussed by us, worried over by us, now going everywhere surrounded by a retinue of ladies and armed guards and being acknowledged by bended knee, deep curtseys and everything beginning 'Your Grace'. I had not realised it would be so difficult. I had not realised how amazing it would be, either, to have a Wydeville presence so firmly in place that all had to acknowledge the rest of us, whether they liked it or not. I was more than sure they did not. But, that was their problem, not ours. The king had chosen; the king had imposed a Wydeville widow on them as his queen and they had to live with it, all of them. It was a good feeling. It was recompense for all the snide comments about 'foreign duchesses' which I had overheard a few times, about 'Wydevilles coming in the back door' – reference to Antony marrying Elizabeth Scales, oh yes, the gossip mongers were out in full force before this royal wedding. They had to eat their words and I trusted they tasted right bitter, too.

Chapter Eleven

During the Twelve Days of Christmas, her first as Queen, Elizabeth came up with a scheme to put her brother Antony in front of everyone. It was a deliberate 'you will take notice of the Wydevilles' action and the kind of thinking I approved of. It was worthy of my own scheming. I was proud of her.

She decided to set up an emprise, a chivalric happening, which would result in a big show piece occasion with the eyes of London on him. She consulted me on it and we discussed it long and seriously before asking Edward if he approved. It was pretty much a tournament, a knight against a knight, joust, battle, all show and yet an actual fight. Elizabeth was sure Edward would agree, if there was one thing he liked above all it was the joust, the pitting of one knight against another, two men perfectly matched, a good fight, a good challenge. He did not know at that time it was a scheme on her part to detract him from the small fact that she had not become pregnant. She had decided she would not bear a child until she had a big showy coronation to make up for the hasty secretive marriage. We had ways of preventing conception, quite a few, actually, she chose the small sponge and it worked.

Edward wholeheartedly accepted the idea of the emprise and so it was planned, step by step. My ladies checked with Antony's tailor to get the exact size of the collar that was needed, Elizabeth used the royal jeweller to make it, she and her ladies concocted the 'rules' for the emprise and she wrote it, in a very elegant hand indeed, on a small scroll. And we went over and over the plans to present it to him. It worked to perfection.

After Mass one day, we were at Shene, as I recall, Antony approached his sister, going down on one knee as he always did, his bonnet off his head. As I said, he was better at the deference thing than Richard and I were. We had to think about it, he didn't. Elizabeth's ladies fluttered around him and fastened a collar round his right thigh. It carried a flower of souvenance, remembrance, and indicated an emprise. Whilst he was busy thinking about that, one of them dropped the small scroll into his bonnet. He discovered that when he went to put the bonnet back on his head. Elizabeth had carefully tied it with gold thread and sealed it with her personal seal.

Antony was a seasoned courtier and knew what to do. He did not open it himself, although he must have been burning up with curiosity. He took it to Edward and asked if he would open it for him. A courtier was requested to read it aloud to all who happened to be there.

It was simple. Antony had been commanded, by order of his Queen, to arrange a tournament in the City of London, to last two days. The command was for him to fight on horseback and on foot a noble knight of equal standing to himself. He was delighted; it was just the sort of thing he revelled in as well. Edward gave formal permission for the emprise to go ahead and Antony went away to work out who he would challenge. It gave him something to do and the courtiers as well; they were full of ideas and suggestions. It ran round the court like flames eating old rushes, everyone was interested and wanted to ask about it. The first part of the thinking behind the emprise was working; everyone wanted to speak to a Wydeville.

Antony, after much discussion with everyone – I think to make them all feel part of it - eventually chose Lord Anton, Earl of Bevere and Beveresse, otherwise known as the Bastard of Burgundy. Big man, apparently, a fearless fighter. Everyone said 'good choice' and looked forward to the battle. Unfortunately it didn't happen for an age for one reason and another, Lord Anton was kept busy fighting real battles and having problems, then there was the question of safe passage. All right, I thought, it's under way, it will happen, let's think about other things until it actually occurs.

1465 was a year of high points for the Wydevilles, for even as we worked on the emprise, so the plans were going ahead for the next big occasion. Edward had finally agreed his Queen could have a coronation.

It seemed as if I was hardly at home for the first six months of that year, rushing hither and thither, working out lists of invitations, being measured for gowns, being consulted by my daughter the Queen whilst busy remembering she was my Queen and I had to show all due deference to her ... and at the same time keep in her mind the remainder of her siblings so that influential marriages could be arranged. My beloved Richard was made Treasurer, thus increasing his standing and his duties, for a start. So he was not around much to help.

I want to divert here for a moment. There was an outcry when my son John, then aged 20, married the dowager Duchess of Norfolk, who was about 40 years older than him. Now, I ask you, why did no one raise an outcry when a 17 year old girl was married to a 45 year old Duke? Why is it acceptable that way round and not the other way round? Ah, the hypocrisy of the times ... and the court ... who did not like the Wydevilles and did not think that one through to its logical conclusion. It was arranged; I admit that, but again there was a love bond and my son was very happy with his wife.

There were murmurings going on all the time. I heard them, ignored them, but I stored it all for the future. They should have known that ... fools that they were. I heard how we had 'deserted' the Lancastrian cause and become Yorkists; I heard how we 'pushed out' trusted Yorkists, Clarence, Warwick, Gloucester...

My answer to them - then and now - is this: rubbish. Gloucester was busy with the north of England where he held sway in his brother's name and none dared touch him. Clarence was wealthy beyond belief, creating close ties with Warwick to the extent that during the time the court was not discussing the Wydevilles they were discussing the connection between the two and wondering what was going on. It was well known that Warwick was more than angry over Edward's secret marriage and the consequent destruction of his dynastic plans and dreams. And so... tell me now how the Wydevilles pushed aside trusted Yorkists. One brother was busy with his own empire building, another was empire building with the third one and we, former Lancastrians, had done nothing more than switch sides, which three quarters of those in court had done at some time or another. We all knew where our fortunes lie, with the one who is on the throne at the time. We just happened to have been bolder than they were in getting where we wanted to go. Jealousy, pure jealousy is the reason for the hostility we generated. The big problem is, it didn't go away.

My scrying bowl was in Grafton and I needed, desperately, to look into the future. After cautiously asking around, I was given the name of a wise woman in London and went in secret and in disguise to see her. She lived in two rooms in a building off Red Lion Square, warm, well furnished and comfortable. She was very old, with a face so wrinkled it was hard to see the woman she once was. Her hair was sparse and completely white, twisted up into a bun on the back of her head. Her voice, though, was pure and strong, the voice of a young woman. She did not know who I was; I used Antony's wife's name to arrange my visit. I wanted to keep a shield between us; I was afeared that my name would prevent her giving me what I wanted to know. She was no Clary, there was no trance communication and I did not feel a sense of kinship with her. That is not to denigrate her abilities, for she was both perceptive and accurate. Her first words were: 'why have you come to me, my lady, when you know well how to find your own answers from the spirit side of life?'

"Sometimes I need someone else to read for me so I know what I am receiving is right," I said in response.

She nodded. "That I understand well. We can be blinded by our own visions. Where then is your bowl?"

I was not surprised she knew I used a scrying bowl. "In Northamptonshire, a good distance from here. I had not planned on staying in London so long. I need to return home and begin scrying again."

She sat for a moment, eyes closed, fingers entwining in her lap. When she spoke again, there was an odd echo to her voice, as if it was coming through something, a tunnel of some kind. Not quite a trance but as if someone else speaking through her. I had my experiences with Clary to show me the difference, which was so subtle not everyone would pick up on it. It was her and yet not quite her.

"Yes. Your guide awaits you. He has been patient this long time but now is impatient to speak with you. Your days are too full and your nights too weary to connect with him. I would ask you to return home as soon as you can, before you lose the contact. Not through his leaving you but through your own closing down."

I felt the dread of death go through me at her words and knew she was right. I was closing down, I had not seen anything in an age and my heart ached for the contact.

Incautiously, I said, "I will. The moment this coronation is over."

"Ah, you are invited, I take it."

"Yes, I am." Sigh of relief, she still did not know who I was, only that I was aristocracy and was well thought of enough to be invited.

"It will be a fine occasion. Nothing will mar it. The Queen will become with child the same night and the king will be content. The people murmur against this Queen and her family but they murmur wrongly. The king chose her of his own free will. The country will have to live with his choice."

"Are there – problems ahead for the family?" I had to ask.

"My lady, there are always problems ahead. No life is without problems but I have to say that the family who married into the Yorks will find many problems that are not of their own making. They will be caught up in the tide of events that the Yorks have set in motion without knowing they have done so. I see conflict, I see treason, I see deception, I see loyalty."

"Do you see – death?"

"The Reaper ever stands at our side, my lady. Of course there is death, it is part of life. I am not being shown who or where – that will be for you to discover if it is related to you in any way."

"I thank you." I was disheartened and encouraged by her words at the same time. I always knew there would be problems: in a time such as this, where strife is constant and power play inevitable, there had to be conflict, there had to be deception, but treason? That was a big word and a big step for anyone to take. I wondered who she could be referring to and wondered if I would be told, if I could find the quiet time to scry. Somehow I doubted it. So much is hidden from us, so much we have to discover as we walk our pathway step by step.

She spoke for some time on generalities, designed to soothe but they were welcome, balm to my troubled mind. Comfort and love for my family, health for myself and my husband, positions of power for us all. She spoke of the greenness of Northamptonshire and accurately spoke of my love for the area and the house in which I lived. Then she said:

"My lady, my guide is saying to you, go home as soon as you can. Go home and be quiet in your mind. Find the time to sit and meditate, find the time to look into your bowl. But he is also saying, do not bring that bowl to London, whatever you do."

I caught my breath, for I had been thinking of doing just that.

"You cannot be seen with such a thing in the heart of England. There are those who will hold this against you, those who will call you witch and other names, those who will seek to bring you down should they discover your abilities. Leave the bowl at your home in the country. Go there to consult. But before you do any of that, go to your home here this night and be quiet and ask your guide to come to you. There is much you need to talk about if you are to walk the pathway without too many problems."

Just as Clary had done many times, the old lady fell silent, blinked a few times and coughed. When she spoke again, her voice had returned to normal. She had definitely been used by someone to speak to me and it had been very revealing, if equally unrevealing. There was much I had to find out for myself. I offered her a gold coin, which she took with obvious but not obsequious gratitude, which I liked.

"You are a talented seer, my lady. You can find your own answers. But I understand the need for someone else to confirm it for you. Be at peace in your heart. You have done all you can for those you love. You care for the family, that is clear but now it is for them to find their own way through life."

I left her with many thoughts tumbling through my mind. I respected her as a seer and knew she was right about the bowl and my abilities. I had to keep them under lock and key in my heart and mind, be careful who I spoke to, if at all, about any of it. Elizabeth hadn't mentioned my scrying or anything else for a long time and that pleased me. The less she thought about it, the less likely she would be to talk to Edward about it.

Conflict, treason, the words spun in my head. I could not see my way through them. There was no time to go back to Grafton, not yet anyway. I had a coronation to attend.

But I had that night to talk to my guide.

I got the peace I needed to speak to my guide only after spending a considerable amount of time with Elizabeth, who was agonising over who to appoint to do this and that, would Antony be happy to be cup-bearer, would Clarence be willing to do this and someone else to do that and what about her gown and what head dress should she wear and who should be her attendants in order of seniority more than those she actually liked and could she include her sisters and … my head was reeling when I finally got to my rooms, the ones she had given me. They were luxurious in the extreme, furnished with heavily carved furniture and hung with very rich tapestries that must have taken months to complete. I loved them. Fit for a Queen's mother, I thought. But that night I was too anxious for quiet, if that isn't a nonsensical statement, to appreciate them as I normally did.

Richard was not there. He was still out with whoever he had meetings with that evening, Hastings or someone. I threw off my cloak, dismissed the maid and went to sit by the window, looking out at buildings and more buildings. London, crammed full of houses and people. I sat picturing instead the calming greens and browns of Northamptonshire. Of all the homes we had, the Bury was the one which I loved best, the one where I felt completely relaxed and content. I closed my eyes and began to walk through the much-loved rooms in my mind. I was actually there. It calmed me.

It was then I sensed my guide coming close and looking disapprovingly at me. "All right," I said, "I know, I've been so busy with this and that but nothing so important that I could not give you the time you wanted. Apologies."

"Someone is here to speak with you." My guide was calmness itself. I had become aware of another presence, but it was only when I smelled the fresh flowers that I knew it was Clary. I felt my heart fill with happiness.

"I have not deserted you, my lady." Her calm quiet voice filled my head and I smiled.

"I didn't really believe for a moment you had, Clary. I miss you."

"You do not have to miss me. I am always with you. I went back to the other side so I could walk with you. Did you not realise that?"

"No. These things are new to me."

"Not so. You know - and accept - we all have a time to return to our home beyond the veil. You have said so. I had my time to return, too. We all go back at a certain time for a reason. I had fulfilled my purpose on your side, helped all the people I could help, including you, my lady. You paid for my burial; I will never forget that. No one else would have done such a thing. I have a proper grave in a quiet corner and for that I am so grateful. You know well that the body does not matter once the spirit has left it but there is peace of mind in knowing where that body lies."

"It was but a small token of my thanks."

"I had done little but encourage that which you already had within you. Your abilities would have surfaced sooner or later."

"Maybe, but you were there to help when I needed it most."

"No meeting is by chance. It was the right time for us both. Now, let me say this. You chose well when you went to see the wise woman this day. Her guide is ancient and knows much. There are problems to come, but I will be there. Be aware of the flowers and know I will be there and will help as much as I can."

In that moment Grafton disappeared and I was back in London, busy, bustling, power hungry London and Richard was walking in the door, his cloak over his arm, looking weary and elated at the same time.

I went to greet him, wondering how long both of us could carry the worries and cares of this momentous occasion, how long it would be before we could both return to Grafton and recuperate. Odd thought, we were not ill but I felt we would be if we did not have some respite from it all.

We went to bed that night and made love somewhere around dawn. I woke needing Richard and he seemingly woke needing me. I had hardly opened my eyes when I felt him pressing against me. I thought at first he was sleeping but no, those beautiful eyes I loved so much were wide open and staring at me with pure lust. The look was matched with a loving but licentious smile. I did not complain.

I had two thoughts: one was, I hoped I did not start breeding again, I was about done with producing offspring and the other was, could anyone think of a better way to start a day?

Chapter Twelve

THE coronation. The only one that mattered to me. Margaret of Anjou's had been a lively but somehow soulless ceremony, as if everyone was saying everything by rote. Margaret had been calm, almost icy, acting as if it was her God given right to be crowned Queen.

May 26th 1465. Note it. Note it well. That was the day the Wydevilles truly arrived. Oh, we were well known by then, the upstart family who had somehow coerced a handsome, smiling and most of all young king to marry their eldest daughter, albeit she was stunningly beautiful and obviously fertile, but being known was one thing, marriage or not, being crowned Queen was another thing entirely. And what a coronation Edward had agreed to have for her! Triumphal procession, decorated streets, the whole thing from start to finish was expensive, showy, dramatic, just what she - and the family - needed.

It was so fraught, though, I wondered if any of us would survive the days. Antony, fortunately, had his lovely calm wife to advise on his clothes, which bonnet would best flatter his face, the trappings for his horse, whether to carry this sword or that, all the things men fuss about, whilst she quietly got on with choosing a design for her gown and getting her seamstress to go ahead with it, without consulting him. Elizabeth Scales had wisdom beyond her years when it came to dealing with men. I thought my Elizabeth could learn from her, if they could be together for a while. But then again, would my daughter want to change? It was the way Edward knew her and the way it seemed he cared for her, so perhaps she was best left as the wildcat I knew she could be when roused, either in anger or in passion, with the other sides of her left to show themselves according to the company she was in, everything from a simpering shy girl to the dominant woman who demanded attention be paid to her. I knew my daughter well and knew how much like me she was, in many ways.

I consulted with Richard endlessly on what he wanted to wear for the day, whilst following Elizabeth Scales' example and getting my own gown created without telling anyone what it was.

The coronation ceremonies began on the 24th, went through the 25th but really the 26th was the culmination of my dreams, hopes and prayers.

On the 24th, wearing one of her new beautiful gowns, Elizabeth started her journey to Westminster Palace. Edward had played his part in the proceedings by appointing another group of Knights of the Bath, a highly sought after knighthood. After that he went back to the Palace and – what? Entertained himself with his friends and courtiers, no doubt, whilst his queen held the attention of most of London on her victorious journey to the crown that was hers. Forgive me, it is still the most exciting thing that ever happened to us – or ever will.

There was my daughter; her hair caught up in a net sparkling with gems, cascading down her back in all its silver glory. The sun shone on it, making it look even brighter than it was. Her dress, of cloth of silver set with gems, shone in the sunshine too. The Mayor, Aldermen and all the dignitaries of London met her at a place called Shooters Hill and with this esteemed escort, every one of them wearing their very best clothes, she rode in great style through Southwark, through the elegant buildings of Gracechurch Street to the Tower, where she stayed overnight in the royal lodgings. What she felt is anyone's guess, elated, excited, flattered, appreciated, loved? I heard that the people called out to her, offered blessings for her, throwing petals down for the procession to ride on. She told me later that her face ached from smiling so much for so long. That was her part to do, I could not be there, I had to be patient and wait to talk to her when she eventually arrived at the Palace of Westminster. I knew the clothes, though, for we had laboured long over what she was to wear and what jewels went with which gown.

Saturday, in yet another new gown, this one of sapphire blue with sapphires in her hair and round her neck, she was escorted into the city through Cheapside and many other streets lined with people, with the new Knights of the Bath leading the way. Two of her brothers were among them; Richard and John had been knighted. My cup truly runneth over, I thought.

More people, more cheering, more adulation and acceptance. Then she arrived at Westminster Palace where she was to stay overnight, to prepare herself for the coronation the next day.

I was waiting for her in her rooms when she arrived. She threw herself into my arms, weeping with happiness at the way she had been cheered by the crowd, tired from all her emotions, ears ringing from the noise of the people, the horses, the clatter of arms and armed men and the simple fact that she had been alone in the middle of it, to all intents and purposes. Queen Consort she might be but that day she had been without the king, just a woman alone before the massed crowd of Londoners who, fortunately, had accepted her.

I hugged her and then led her to a couch. She sat down, leaned back and almost immediately fell asleep. I instructed her ladies to take care of her and went to supervise food and drink to be there the moment she woke and to ensure her coronation gown was pressed and ready for her to put on in the morning. I had to busy myself to wind down my emotions. I had no chance to sleep then, as she did, for there were still things to do, decisions to be made, orders to be given. When that was all done, I went to find my husband, for I had no intention of being a lady alone on such a momentous occasion. I needed his arms, his lips, his loving eyes and gentle voice to quieten me and convince me that all this was not a dream from which I would wake and find that we were still the struggling for attention Wydevilles with a simple home in Grafton, which was for some, the middle of nowhere.

What can I tell you of the ceremony, I wonder? More than that, how can I tell you of the ceremony? The magnificence of the abbey is beyond my power to describe, the solemnity of the occasion, the anointing with oil, the presentation of the sacred relics, the voices chanting and singing praises to God, the sound filling the huge vaulted ceiling and banging against the walls until I thought I would literally burst asunder with pride and the need, the overwhelming desire - which I fought by biting my lips until they all but bled - to stand up and shout THIS IS MY DAUGHTER!

I could not have done such a thing at such a moment but the Lord God knows how much I wanted to! Elizabeth looked utterly magnificent in a gown of cloth of gold with a long train carried by several high ranking ladies who were dressed in glorious colours and gems and attended by knights more glorious than the ladies, with their slashed doublets and jewelled bonnets, their shining boots and their beringed hands. I clutched Richard's arm so hard he had bruises for days but he never complained once or tried to remove my hand, either, so I knew he was as moved by it as I was. When Elizabeth, the Queen, no less, how hard it was to comprehend that still, walked anywhere, under the canopy of purple silk, it was as if the whole elaborate ceremony, from start to finish, from entrance in the abbey to the final cup at the banquet, had been arranged for her and no other. But then this is a proud mother speaking, not an onlooker who might have seen it all before. I know this; Elizabeth's sheer joy at being Queen outshone Margaret of Anjou's in every possible way. No cheerless dull acceptance of a status she thought was due to her but a singing happiness that it had happened, that she had got that far, that she had been given this splendid ceremony and dramatic procession, been given the banquet and the rejoicing, she, a Lancastrian widow with no prospects and no assets but her stunning looks and her two boys as evidence of her fertility. We will not speak of the other one, whose memory lingered with me throughout that magnificent day. I wanted to say haunted but he was very much alive, as far as I knew, anyway.

I sat at the table, almost unable to eat but able to drink – for which I was grateful – with the elevated among the aristocracy. I was on a special table set aside for ladies and the newly created knights. Me, Jacquetta Wydeville, was there with the Duchess of Buckingham and the Countess of Essex, thinking I was there by right of being Duchess of Bedford as well as the Queen's mother, feeling more than proud by this time, when I became aware of the hint of fresh flowers. There were none on the table. I sent out a thought to Clary, knowing she was there and got back the impression of someone quite overwhelmed with the grandeur of it all. I looked at the great hall, the mass of people, Clarence wearing a doublet of what looked like cloth of gold, riding around on a white charger, I heard the noise, the confusion of voices and clatter of dishes and goblets and realised just how momentous the whole thing was. I sent back a 'thank you' to Clary for showing me the other side of the coronation. It was one thing to be a proud mother and elevated aristocrat, quite another to be a humble working woman who had never seen such wealth and opulence in her life. It was good for me to see the other side, to remind me that there were hundreds, thousands of people who would never see this kind of life. It was a humbling experience.

I knew Elizabeth was over tired and anxious to be with her husband. By convention he had stayed away from the coronation, so I was aware she was glad when the ceremonials eventually wound down. Antony looked tired and professed himself grateful when it was over so he and his wife could return to the calm of Norfolk and their bucolic life together. I went to my bed that night exhausted with the emotion of it all and was content just to be in my husband's arms. My sleep was disturbed with strange dreams of processions of odd-looking men and women, some with animal heads. I woke several times, dismissing the dreams, going back to sleep and finding myself in another similar one. I vowed not to drink so much next time but to eat more instead.

And so my daughter was officially crowned Queen of England.

And now let me quash a very silly story that began circulating within hours of the coronation and which persists to this day.

No people came from Luxembourg to protest about the coronation. Antony did not fight each one of them and drive them back to their ship; in fact he never left the hall once. His task was Cup-bearer and this he did with style and grace. Where that nonsensical report came from I do not know, nor do I care. It was false and that was all there was to it.

Think about it, I am Luxemburg aristocracy, why would 'my people' come and complain about one of their own being made Queen of England? And, why would they wait so long before coming? They had all the time before she was crowned to make their feelings known, if they had any. This was in direct contradiction of the letters of congratulation I received from my family back there when the news spread to Europe, as it inevitably did, after all, this was the King of England getting married! Oh my, I do wonder why people have nothing better to do than come up with these strange, outlandish stories!

No, that's wrong. I do know why. It is anything, absolutely anything at all, to throw at the Wydevilles. They would prefer rocks but lacking those or evidence to provide the rocks, they make do with a pack of lies, no matter how nonsensical those lies might be.

As soon as we could reasonably do so, Richard and I departed for Grafton, there to rest from the exertions of the coronation, that is, the planning and the actual event itself.

It felt as if we had been gone for an age, not just a month or two. I was more than content to wander round the much-loved rooms, ostensibly checking on everything but actually re-acquainting myself with my home. I brushed my hand over the scrying bowl, silently saying 'later' for there were instructions to give and a meal to eat and all the usual demands which got in the way of what I really wanted to do, be quiet and calm and look into the future.

As we sat eating our meal, our first at the Bury in what felt like forever, Richard suddenly said: "did you realise Warwick was not at the coronation?"

I hadn't and I said so. In the chaos and confusion of the days, a swirling montage of colour, noise, excitement and what seemed like hundreds of people, Warwick had been far from my mind. Perhaps if I had seen him his presence would have registered – no, change that, had I seen him his presence would definitely have registered, you do not miss the Earl whose stature and personality made him an outstanding figure, but he was not there and so I had concentrated on those who were.

"Edward sent him off on some commission or other," Richard continued, with a smile. "If you think about it, Edward chose the guests well, didn't he?"

132

And he had. They had come from all loyalties and the one who might possibly have caused discord was quietly sent away, no doubt on something important but for all that, he had been sent from court on a major occasion. I thought that did not bode well, it would be something that would rankle in the Earl's mind.

Dismissing the thought, I said, "now we are properly established, I can work at getting the remainder of our brood married off."

Richard laughed. "Do you never stop scheming, wife of mine?"

"No!" I retorted. "Someone has to!"

"I'm glad of that," he said quietly. "It's not something I could do."

Eventually, through diplomacy and tact and currying favours here and there, I am proud to report that my children married well.

Can any proud mother ask for more than that her children marry well? I would have wished Richard and Edward had married but so be it, I could not force them into matrimony if it was not their wish. Edward was everything he was foreseen to be, ever adventuring. No wife would have remained happy with him as husband, I must admit!

That night, under pretext of wanting to pray alone for a time, I went to my scrying bowl to see what it would tell me.

There were visions showing immediately, as if it had been waiting for me to return. I saw Elizabeth with a child in her arms, as the wise woman had prophesied. I saw Clarence and Warwick together then merging into one, which I did not understand. I saw conflict again, not so much a battle as some kind of dispute, I saw Richard and I at the Bury and in court and then the water went black. Again I was being shut out; the message was I had seen enough.

That night, before going to sleep, I asked my guide to speak with me, to tell me if there was anything I needed to know. He repeated the Clarence/Warwick melting together and told me to watch out for that. Then he told me not to worry, that all would be well and I fell asleep, a proper sleep for the first time in weeks.

Whatever was to come, it was there and I had to live it. No point in worrying about it was my last thought before going into what I believe was a dreamless sleep.

Chapter Thirteen

Life was quiet for a while, if you can ever call Court life quiet. There were the usual intrigues, plots and rumours going around, most of which anyone could simply ignore or laugh off but there were always elements, nuggets of truth which could not be discounted.

The first 'legitimate' royal child, a girl, was born in February 1466, without any problem at all. The child was named Elizabeth and Edward professed to be pleased with the new arrival. If he was disappointed not to have a son immediately he did not show it. To my great pleasure, I was chosen to be godmother and was even more pleased when I found out that the other godmother was to be Cecily, duchess of York.

I realise I have not mentioned this formidable lady very much in my narrative so far, but I should, for she was a great presence in court – and out of it. Her word seemed to be law as far as her sons were concerned. Kings or princes, they obeyed her, for the most part. This was because no matter what anyone thought – and there were many who tried to cast aspersions on her character and her wisdom – she was infinitely wise and sensible and people did listen to her.

One story that did the rounds for some time was that she had committed adultery with some archer or other and that Edward was the result. I want to say here and now, as loudly as I can, as far as I am concerned that was - and is - absolute rubbish. That's the second time I've said something was rubbish in a very short time, but it goes to show how people love to spread stories about those in high places and even those not in such high places, too. Court was a seething hotbed of innuendo and outright lies on a daily basis. The trick was to dissect the lies and find the truth behind them, which had invariably been distorted. Let me say this. Lady Cecily, as far as I could tell – remember I had visions beyond the 'normal' person in court at that time – had a love for her husband as deep and as vast and as all encompassing as mine was for my husband. I would not for a moment consider even looking at another man in that way, let alone actually do it. She was the same. A proud, dignified, quiet lady with authority in her voice and sense in her head, that sums up Cecily of York. She did not entirely approve of me or of my daughter. She was unhappy with the marriage, that I knew. But then, so was virtually every person in court at that time. It was something we knew and accepted and decided to live with. We met one afternoon in her chambers to discuss the baptism and our relationship, at her request. It was an informal but cool meeting. I knew we would never be friends in the accepted sense of the word, but we came to an understanding. Her son, who happened to be the king at the time, had chosen my daughter, who happened to be the widow of a Lancastrian, and married her. There was nothing either of us could do about it; we had to live with it. I was happy, of course, at the elevation of my family, she was not happy because she too had desired a dynastic marriage for her son. We both knew what the other was thinking and feeling, nothing had to be said. We were cordial and polite and parted on amicable terms. It was the closest we would get to being on good terms. We were in accord on one thing, though, the latest arrival was a beautiful baby and would grow up to do wonderful things. As all grandmothers do, we saw nothing but good for our little one.

I consulted my scrying bowl that night, asking first for illumination on Lady Cecily and was shown her standing in the middle of a battlefield, conflict raging all around her and she a point of calm within it. That did not bode well for the future but it did show her role in court life. I asked about the newest arrival, the baby Elizabeth, and was shown a smiling happy child wearing a crown. I was taken aback at that, but then smiled and thought, life had many twists and turns and it could well be that she would make a dynastic marriage in the future. After all, she was the daughter of a king, was she not? He would be able to arrange such a union for her. A Wydeville carrying on the royal line! The thought was both exciting and comforting. The bowl would show me nothing else that night. I wished it had, there was much I still wanted to know.

Oh yes, there's another story I need to quash as well, whilst I am busy spoiling the fun of everyone by destroying their heartfelt myths and beliefs about us Wydevilles. Much as I wanted to throw off the conventions which bound me, the shutting myself away to have a child, the churching ceremony afterwards, that kind of thing, and at times did break the rigid rules of how many days I had to be secluded, a Queen cannot do that. Every eye is on her, every mouth ready to talk about her if she does anything 'different'. After the birth of Elizabeth, her first child with Edward, we had the churching service and a banquet. I knelt by her side. Several times she bid me rise and then I knelt again.

Now I know that 'some observers' reported back to their masters, whoever they happened to be, that my daughter had grown so haughty she even had her own mother kneel before her. As with every such comment, it found its way back to England.

I know that 'some observers' did not like the Wydevilles and anything which they could use to denigrate the Queen or any of the family was fair game to them. But they were - and are - totally wrong. I insisted on deference at all times to those above us in rank, it was inculcated into my children and so it was into me, too. My daughter was Queen. I knelt before her. Does anyone want to argue with that? What you don't do is ask me how I felt about it…

137

One by one the family left the Bury. One by one they departed and left the home to the servants, the horses, the dreams and aspirations of one mother for her brood and one exciting man, my husband. I could not get enough of him at that time, his arms, his kisses, his body. He was still travelling hither and thither on this business or that, he had titles galore and things to do that took him away from me. During those times I went to court to stop myself bemoaning his absence. I kept asking myself what was the matter with me, we had been married for an age, we were supposed to be old and comfortable with one another, we were not supposed to act like newly weds. Gracious, even Antony and Elizabeth acted more sedately than Richard and I did, but I could not help it and I don't think he could, either. We were the same toward each other as the day we married, it never changed. My man, my love, my life. When I asked the bowl about him, it remained stubbornly blank, which upset me considerably. I realised then that at times we have to walk the path blindly, whether we like it or not.

That year Richard was appointed Treasurer. Unfortunately, for that to happen, someone had to relinquish the position and it happened to be Sir John Tiptoft who had to take step back. He was not someone you wanted as an enemy. It roused a lot of bad feeling in a lot of people, I almost said, 'bad people' there but changed my mind. They weren't bad, just loyal to whoever it was they felt deserved it. I could not deny them that.

Elizabeth fell for a baby again, as I knew she would, for she was extremely fertile, with the right man. Edward was definitely the right man, if the accounts of his 'other' children were anything to go by. She declared she didn't care about them, the children she had were royal, which was all that mattered. And so life ticked on reasonably quietly, with my only disquiet being the whereabouts of Margaret of Anjou and the ever closer relationship between Clarence and Warwick, which seemed to me to be unhealthy. I was not the only one; it was the talk of court, in undertones as no one dared to say it out loud. Well, for sure they could not do that, he was a prince of the royal blood after all and Edward's heir, until the marriage to my daughter.

In saying that, I realised with a shock where the problem originated. Clarence had been disinherited by Edward's marriage. Now, if that were me … I would have been outright furious at being disinherited, would wish the fires of hell on the head of the person who had been chosen instead of me … and I would go seek the companionship and understanding of someone who had been equally disinherited, in a manner of speaking, by the same act. Warwick had been deprived of his role as kingmaker, his diplomatic advances left in tatters and he looking foolish in the eyes of those he had approached … no matter which way I looked at it, there was trouble looming. Richard agreed with me.

"The simple fact is," he said one night, musing as we sat by a fire with mulled wine and sugared fruits as our treat, "Edward was not destined to be a king who did not have a Queen. One way or another he would have found someone to marry. If he had not chosen himself Warwick would have done it for him and then Clarence would have been disinherited."

"I heard that he was made duke of Clarence when he was twelve," I pointed out. "That's a long time to believe you are next in line, no matter what logic comes into it. Someone surely mentioned this to him at some time but when you're young and see a glittering life ahead of you, do you believe them?"

Richard shook his head. "Of course not. We were all young and innocent and blinded by what we believed was rightly ours, weren't we? Few people have the image of the crown of England held out to them at such a young age. No wonder he took it so hard."

"Warwick had much to lose, too. His reputation for one and that counts for a lot in a man with his standing."

"It is a deadly combination," he agreed. "Edward should be looking out for trouble."

"Is he?"

"No. He's confident of the loyalty of his brother and his cousin. If there's trouble, it will be an abrupt awakening for our liege lord."

Did I care about that? Yes, but only insofar as it affected my precious daughter and her children. Edward, I thought, was big enough and handsome enough to take care of himself but my daughter was not the tough lady she sometimes made herself out to be.

Chapter Fourteen

And then we were into 1467 and the emprise was finally to take place. It felt as if many years had passed since Elizabeth had put the scheme into effect, had raised everyone's expectations of a great show and a valiant fight, but in truth it was no more than two years, such was the pressure of everything that had happened in the intervening period.

Antony had the devil's own job to secure safe passage for Lord Anton, the sea being infested, there is no other word for it, with pirates who were after anything under sail in the hope of good bounty. But he was as persistent as me when something important was at stake and messages were sent back and forth across the water until an eight month safe passage was granted. Then we could heave a sigh of relief and get on with the next part of the emprise. The planning.

I did not begin to appreciate how big this thing was until I was asked to help with the organisation.

The foundation was there: Lord Anton v. Lord Scales, Smithfield, summer.

From there on, though, decisions had to be made on a thousand things: where would Lord Anton arrive, who would meet him, where would he stay when he arrived, where would he stay when he reached London, how many would he bring with him, was there sufficient stabling for the horses he would doubtless have with him, was there a secret place he could practice before the tournament and finally, what gifts should be bought for him as a thank you for taking part in the emprise.

Antony, where would he be when Lord Anton arrived, where would he stay in London, did he need a secret place to practice before the tournament.

Edward, where would he be when this all happened and which route would he take into London. There were questions such as, would he want to go to St

Paul's and make an offering and what sort of procession did he want. What roads needed to be secured for this procession and what roads would need to be secured for the arrival of Lord Anton and Antony at the field on the two days of the tournament. How many men at arms would be needed for protection on the journeys into London and the two day event, too. Who would get the commission to build the staging for the spectators and the lists? Who would get the task of making the pavilions for the two men? What sort of display would Antony make when he entered the field. Who would he get to make the weapons…

That was how it went. Every time we resolved one thing, another came up to be resolved. Some were easy, some were not. What I thought of as the basics were easy, workmen were put on standby to build the staging and the lists when the order was given. Staff were put on standby to cook for Lord Anton and his entourage, no matter how many there were and given a prepared list of foods and places they could go to buy it when the time came. Stabling was arranged for hundreds of horses, both Lord Anton's and Antony's. All that kind of decision making was relatively easily done and disposed of, leaving the bigger ones to be confronted, such as, did Antony need a new suit of armour for the fight?

"But of course!" he said, as if there had been any question of it.

What sort of display did he have in mind to enter the field?

"Horses," he told us, 'us' being his father, his wife, his brothers Edward, John and Richard and his counsellors, squires and advisers. Clarence stopped by often, as Antony had asked him to carry his helm into the field, which he said he was proud to do. I think he was enjoying the planning as much as the rest of us were. He had some good ideas which contributed

142

considerably to the end result. Edward asked to be kept in the discussions too. It was quite an experience, the whole planning thing.

In the end it was decided there would be nine horses, all elaborately decorated, with different drapes and ornamentation for the two days. That was enough to keep anyone busy from that moment until the day of the tournament, as it involved a good deal of detailed work. Pages, yes, we decided, all identically dressed, to ride the horses. That had to be designed. Then there was Antony's outfits for the two days, including what he would wear on his triumphant journey to London – "by barge," he told us. "I've decided I'll wait at Grenewich until my opponent arrives and then come into London by barge. I can have a horse waiting for me at St Katherines or Blackfriars. What do you think?"

What I thought was, this was an occasion like no other. The cost was astronomical, the detail and planning beyond belief, the excitement higher and more contagious even than the Coronation and that had been exhausting enough. Antony and his father were like children at Christmas, both revelling in the intricacies and politics of it all as children would the mummers, the feasting and the gifts. They spent ages discussing who to invite to carry the weapons, who would do this and who would do that. I was caught up in it all, thinking of how it would reflect gloriously on the Wydevilles, when Antony brought me down to earth with a bump.

"I'll have my physician and surgeon standing by," he said, almost nonchalantly, "in case I'm injured."

It was only then I fully realised that this was not just a contest, but an actual fight with weapons that could maim or even kill. I hoped Edward would stop it if it looked as if it was going that far but – accidents happen, in jousts and tourneys, accidents happen and people are injured and killed. I came over faint in that moment but Elizabeth put an arm round me and

143

whispered, "it'll be all right. Antony knows what he's doing. It's a show fight really." I knew it wasn't but I held on to her words for comfort and recovered my equilibrium. But I have to say I did not feel as complacent about the whole thing after that as I had done before the realisation crashed in.

Days passed, days when Antony was at Grenewich, doing heaven alone knows what to pass the time, there are just so many games of Tables you can play after all, while we waited for Lord Anton to arrive. Elizabeth was at Westminster with me, miserable because they were apart, although she tried hard to disguise it. I recognised the great love because it was so like the one I had for my Richard. I thought again, how fortuitous it was that the two had been put together and then laughed to myself. Of course it wasn't fortuitous, as with everything that went on in our lives it had been planned by those beyond the veil. They knew precisely what they were doing.

Messengers arrived – eventually – to say Lord Anton had actually docked at Gravesend. At last, we all sighed, smiled, almost did a dance around the palace; at last we could get this tournament under way. It had only been two years and three months in the planning, by my reckoning, anyway.

I didn't go to see Lord Anton's entry into London. He might well have been a worthy opponent for my son but he wasn't my son so I didn't go and see him. Ah, that sounds petty and full of feminine fluttery nonsense, but it's the truth. Elizabeth and I stayed in the Palace and let him make his grand entrance without the female Wydevilles going to see him. Richard did, he reported back on the man (his opinion, had the look of a fighting man) his entourage (huge, showy, designed to impress) and he thought he was very obviously anxiously awaiting this contest. How he knew this I don't know, unless he had talked to some of Lord Anton's people. He still had every confidence in Antony's ability to win the honour of both days. I just worried. It was nearly as bad as knowing they were going into battle as far as I was concerned. The only difference was this was a showpiece battle, not a life and death one. I hoped.

I confess I got myself invited into the Bishop's Palace to be there when Antony arrived after his triumphant entry into London. He had on a stunning gold gown and his hair was down for a change. I hadn't appreciated how much it had grown. He was wearing gold jewellery set with gems, just enough to look elegant, not so much that it looked ostentatious. I detected Elizabeth's hand in that, it took a woman's eye to create that kind of balance. He looked confident, truly as if nothing would bother him, not even the thought of being in a 'fight' with an accomplished knight and soldier. My son, I thought, full of pride. My golden son. He was everything I had hoped for when he arrived. I briefly wondered whether to tell him of my scrying and my abilities when it occurred to me to go and ask if he would win. Foolish woman that I am, I had been so busy with the details of the whole occasion I had overlooked that small thing. My bowl was in Grafton. I remembered well the words of the wise woman I consulted and had never brought it to London, so I could not use that. I had to just ask and see if I got an answer.

After the celebratory banquet that evening, I went to our rooms before Richard, so I had a little time to be alone. The moment I went in I detected the scent of flowers and knew Clary was waiting for me.

"It has been a while, my lady." I heard her soft voice somewhere round the back of my head. It is hard to explain how I heard her.

"I know. I apologise, I have been-"

145

There was the sense of laughter. Clary did not laugh often but when she did, it was light, reminding me of water tumbling over stones in a shallow fall.

"It matters not. There is no time on this side of the veil. This is a big occasion for your son."

"It is. I so want him to do well."

"He will. Have no fear. No matter what it looks like when they are out there, in the field as you call it, he will do well."

"And make a good show of it?"

"Would you expect him to do anything else?"

In truth, no, I would not. The question did not need to be answered.

"Can I ask, will my daughter the Queen give her husband the heir to the throne he needs?"

There was silence for a moment and then she seemed to sigh. "Yes, but not yet. Be patient, my lady, the son will come."

"I am afeared the king will be impatient."

"The king is not impatient. He is assured of his own virility and his wife's fertility. He also knows daughters are for marrying into rich influential families to create dynasties. My lady, fear not for your daughter. She has her life to lead."

It seemed an odd thing to say. I wanted to ask questions but I felt her fading away from me and I was left with a slightly unsettled feeling. 'Fear not for your daughter.' Did that mean I should fear for my husband, my son or my daughter in law? But then I caught my thoughts up and threw them away. We were discussing my daughter the Queen. I had a direct answer to the questions about my daughter the Queen. We were not discussing anyone else, so the statement could not refer to anyone else, could it?

As if to settle my mind, I felt as if I was being wrapped in a blanket of the softest finest wool imaginable. I sat on the bed, then allowed myself to fall

146

back onto the pillow, the soft feeling still surrounding me. I recognised it eventually as something I had very rarely experienced – peace.

We were all up early next morning. Antony was bustling about before we emerged and we thought we were up with the sun. He was smiling, issuing orders in a calm voice, ensuring that all was as he wanted it, armour, arms, people, horses...

We got ready and set off for Smithfield, leaving Antony to supervise the last of the arrangements needed to allow him to make his dramatic entrance. It was sunny, the streets were crowded with people going about their lives, vendors, merchants, clerics, all bustling here and there and looking busy. We made our way to the City, where the streets were truly crowded with onlookers. There were vendors here too, with pies and bread, water and ale for people to buy to ward off hunger and thirst as they stood eyeing the aristocracy who were arriving for the great tournament.

The field had been well made, that was obvious. It had been Edward's direction that the best people be found and they had been. The staging, one for the ladies, one for the dignitaries of London, one for knights and nobles and one for Edward and his entourage, were very well built. I had been on ones far more rickety than that, one in particular which gave no indication that it was about to collapse in a heap on the ground – but it did. I sat with an Elizabeth on each side of me, one with child, one not. It was still a small sorrow that my son had no legitimate child but it was not something I could help in any way. It was either to be or not - it seemed in this instance it was not to be.

I knew by the roar of the crowd outside that Edward had arrived. He seemed to create that kind of reaction when he went anywhere. Women in particular fell for his charms every time. One smile, one kiss and he had them where he wanted them, usually his followers for life. It was a gift he had and he exploited it to its limit, without seeming to. That was part of his charm. He came in, surrounded by goodness knows how many of his counsellors, squires, pages, messengers and just plain old hangers-on. He was dressed in royal purple and looked every inch the noble king. His laughter could be heard half across the field. He had come to enjoy himself, which was good.

Richard was with John, Edward and a whole crowd of other noble knights, in the staging next to ours. I wanted to wave but the occasion was really too dignified for that kind of behaviour. I controlled the desire and instead played with my fan. He would know the message I was sending by doing that, we had our own private 'language' based on the use of my fan. It is surprising how much you can convey with a few gestures, or even one, come to that.

Men at arms were everywhere, posted at corners of the fences, at the gate, standing in front of the royal stand, their weapons glinting in the sun. It seemed as if sparks of light were shooting in all directions as they moved.

"Isn't my husband handsome?" Elizabeth murmured. She had hardly taken her eyes off him from the moment he arrived. I heard, "God, I want him!" so low she did not really mean it to be overheard. I didn't say a word. That was something I would keep to myself. She shifted restlessly on the seat and I wondered if she needed an extra cushion or something to sit on. Then she stilled and I realised what the problem was. Desire. I was pleased to see it was there, her need for him would help cement the marriage, despite all the opposition to it that I knew was still in the background.

Hated Wydevilles or not, everyone who was anyone had turned out to see a Wydeville challenge another knight this day, under the sun in the field at

Smithfield, in the time honoured way of a battle between two closely matched men. I sent up prayer after prayer that Antony would do well, that honour would come to the Wydevilles from this incredible spectacle. I also silently thanked my daughter for arranging it.

There were shouts out in the street, encouragement I quickly realised, then there was a commotion at the gate and I looked round to see that Antony's grand entrance was about to begin. First came Clarence, superbly dressed as befitted a royal prince, mounted on a beautiful chestnut horse which he was controlling without seeming to do so. Obviously it was a highly trained animal. He had Antony's helm and held it up for all to see. There were high-ranking noblemen with him, each carrying weapons. Then Antony rode in. He looked solemn but assured at the same time. I felt his wife stiffen as she looked at him.

"He's nervous," she whispered to me. "Look at his hands on the reins." He had come without gauntlets and his knuckles were white against the dark leather. It was the only sign of his nervousness and it took someone who knew him well to see it. Everyone else would see the gorgeous animal he rode and the string of horses trotting in after him, each with its elaborate trappings, decoration and magnificent harness. The pages looked superb, chosen by height so they would all look the same as they rode in. He circled the field twice, letting everyone see the glory of the display and then dismounted to make his obeisance to Edward.

His pavilion, fluttering gently in the breeze, was a miracle of silk and gold. He strode over to it as naturally as if it were his home he was entering.

Just in time, too, for Lord Anton had arrived in the field. He had to outdo Antony, of course. I don't know who told him how many horses Antony had arranged to bring with him, but he had twelve, more than equalling Antony's display, each being magnificently decorated.

The crowd outside were roaring encouragement at him, just as they had for my son. That was good to hear.

He went through the obeisance routine and then went to his magnificent pavilion. We sat through the choosing of weapons, the proclamation of the tournament, what to me were tedious conventions but which, judging by the faces of those in the royal stand, were both necessary and right, for they were all watching and listening with rapt attention to it all.

Then both men emerged from their pavilions, fully armoured and looking totally magnificent. They mounted their horses and when the cry was given, they began their run at one another. The spectators held their collective breath, all that could be heard was the jangle – I mean that – of harness and armour and the pounding of the horses' hooves on the sand. Usually a joust is accompanied by the clash of spear or sword on armour, combined with the collective sound of an audience watching every move, shouts and calls, with everyone ready to react when one hit the ground. The first pass, no hits. They wheeled round and ran again. Being equally matched, it was going to be luck as much as skill as to who scored a hit.

No one quite anticipated what would happen in this joust, though. As the two men passed one another, Lord Anton's horse suddenly reared up with a scream of pain that went right through me, then fell to the ground, trapping its rider beneath its heavy body.

Antony immediately wheeled his horse round, his sword held high and rode over to the royal stand where Edward was shouting "Foul!" and shaking his staff. Antony dismounted and, without a word, threw back the trappings on his horse, showing everyone that the saddle was a standard one. Edward sat down, grumbling to himself. I was shocked to think he would even for a moment believe Antony would have an illegal saddle or harness to cause any injury to a horse. I hoped it was the heat of the moment which made him shout like that for everyone to hear. I admired Antony's quick cool thinking. It made him look dignified and made Edward look a little foolish for presuming foul play so readily.

There was a commotion as men at arms rushed to Lord Anton and helped him get free from the animal who had fallen on him. He got to his feet, apparently unhurt but he had been badly winded, for he declined to ride another horse and complete the day's joust. The horse was dead and it was quickly dragged away, leaving the field clear for more jousting. I stayed because I liked to see it, but Elizabeth had already made her way down to the field and into the pavilion, taking advantage of the confusion to circumvent convention and go to her husband. Antony had gone back to take off his armour. My daughter decided to leave too, as she was feeling uncomfortable. They might have planned this day to the very last sequin and inch of gold braid but no one thought of a privy... but that's men for you. Ostentatious display first, practicalities second.

Next day we were back in style as before, decorated horses, glittering armour and weapons, dignitaries, nobles, knights, king, queen, men at arms, heralds, Londoners shouting encouragement at the challengers as they arrived. This time I noticed my daughter had her ladies bring a very thick wrap for her to sit on, so the baby had shifted slightly and was giving her a few uncomfortable moments. I did suggest she rested at home but her reaction was what I really expected:

"This is the final part of the emprise I set up. The least I can do is be there!"

Wydeville to her bones.

After all the ritual had been gone through, announcements, proclamations and endless other detail, the two men confronted one another, carrying battle-axes. They are fearsome weapons and these two were expert with them. From the moment they began what I thought of as the clash, there was no let up between them. Armour was dented and then torn. I dreaded to think what the bruises would be like when they surfaced. The noise of the axes hitting metal combined with the roar of the spectators. Edward was yelling as loud as anyone, caught up in the excitement of it all. Elizabeth had her hands over her eyes, afraid to watch her husband out there in the field, despite it being his big dramatic day. The truth is, as I knew well, one blow could so easily end it all. She was there for support, not to enjoy, in a manner of speaking.

Edward finally threw down his staff to end the fight as it was getting very dangerous, even I could see that, but they fought on before coming to a natural halt. Both men turned and made obeisance to Edward who congratulated them and then, afer a pause, awarded the honour of both days to Antony.

Elizabeth all but shrieked at that point, so delighted she could hardly be still. My daughter smiled a slow, satisfied smile and leaned back against the cushions packed behind her. "They can't say anything about us now, can they?" she said in a voice so low only I heard it. I nodded and smiled back with understanding. "It was a wonderful idea, my dear daughter, a superb idea - and it worked."

"Yes. I knew Antony wouldn't let me down and he didn't." She got up, with her ladies fussing around her and walked down the steps from the staging to cross the field and speak with her husband. Shortly after she left for the Palace, obviously tired but very happy.

Elizabeth, as she had the day before, rushed to Antony's pavilion. It wasn't really acceptable behaviour as I knew it but I understood her need to be with him at that moment and did not doubt his need for her at that time, either.

Another Wydeville victory. They just kept right on coming. I could not have been more pleased.

Chapter Fifteen

Antony's armour, his new armour at that, was badly damaged and he was covered in bruises on his chest, arms, shoulders, even his face wore a bruise for several weeks. It had been a tremendous fight. He was as tired as if he had been in a full scale battle but without the terror that went with it, for Lord Anton had not been out to kill him, just have a good fight. I think they both enjoyed it, if you can say such a thing. From my perspective it was utter madness but still ... I have to say it was a spectacular occasion and really boosted the Wydevilles. Lord Anton returned home with gifts and a reputation as a fearsome fighter. At the celebratory banquet that evening, he professed himself well pleased with the tournament and acknowledged he had been defeated by a better man. That made me even more proud, if that was possible.

A few days later Edward awarded Antony the Lordship of the Isle of Wight. He was still in London recuperating from the battering he took in the tournament, so I got the news much sooner than I would otherwise. I have waited weeks for news of my family, hoping that someone would remember Mother might like to know this piece of news and send a messenger with a letter. I sent letters all the time and got very few back. Did I really expect otherwise? I suppose not.

I was pleased with his new title but I hadn't heard much about the Isle of Wight, so I asked him what he knew about the place. He told me it was a small island off the south coast, apparently it had some pretty villages and a castle and was steeped in history. He was delighted with the honour and was preparing to go there as soon as he and Elizabeth could arrange it. A new place to visit was a gift to Antony, he being someone who loved to explore, alter and build, which is what he planned to do after only his first visit to Carisbrooke

Castle. He came back full of talk of the beauty of the place, the magnificence of the castle which he thought could be made even better and of the quiet easy going ways of the island residents.

His next visit was with a couple of experts and before long great towers were commissioned for the entrance, along with additional accommodation. All this he told me in a non-stop, one-sided conversation aided by drawings which he was showing everyone who would tarry long enough to listen. My son was endlessly enthusiastic about so many things, it was as if his mind could not be satisfied unless he was investigating or working with something different all the time. His range of interests was extensive and, even though I say this as a doting mother, his intellect was amazing. It was a crying shame he didn't have a house full of children, or even one child of his own, he would have been a wonderful father.

I knew Edward, my son that is, not the king, regularly visited Carisbrooke Castle when Antony was there and it was some time before I realised he was the only brother who visited the island. It then occurred to me, after I thought about it, that although John was closer in age to Antony than Edward, he had not been invited. I began to think back and realised that the two who should have been friends, obviously were not. I wondered when that particular division came about and why Edward, the wayward adventurer and soldier son, should be the one Antony had as a friend. I thought often to ask Antony about it but held back. It was his business after all, not mine.

Another royal daughter arrived, a quiet serene beautiful child they named Mary. I was surprised at the surge of emotion I felt when I saw her. After all my children, Elizabeth's two boys and the first royal child, I did not think any baby would stir me to that degree but

155

she did. Elizabeth was happy, Edward said he loved his latest child, life seemed good – for a while anyway. I would have been happier if I could have ignored the feeling that something was going to happen to disrupt the way of life we at that time. The disruption could come from Margaret, from wherever she was scheming and planning, from Warwick who I was sure was scheming and planning, from Clarence, who was smiling and concealing much or from the dark individual himself, Gloucester. I never failed to think of him that way and never did really work out why. It wasn't as if he was a constant presence at court, he spent virtually all his time in the north where he apparently had a reputation second to none as a just, loyal ruler, carrying out his brother's laws and wishes with fairness on all sides. So why did he bother me so much? What was it about him that raised my hackles every time he visited London and I happened to be there? I didn't know and the bowl told me nothing about him.

The court became awash with rumours of Lancastrian plots, which seemed to bother Edward considerably, according to Elizabeth, anyway. To me he was his usual smiling charming self, no hint of underlying concerns to be detected. He was good at masking his feelings, in public at least. I knew he had the Plantagenet temper, there were tales of that, but he didn't show that side to me. But when I saw his outward charm on display, I remembered the flash of temper which he revealed at the tournament, shouting 'Foul!' at Antony before finding out whether it was true. It might have been the heat of the 'battle', it might have been just a bad moment, but it was almost an insult and in that single word he showed his true feelings for the Wydevilles. I had not forgotten it and I knew others had noted it too. I wondered if he regretted his outburst. Giving Antony the Lordship of the Isle of Wight was a big honour, yes, it was a 'congratulations' award, but to me it also said 'sorry about the accusation', not that he would admit it for a moment. A king did not have to apologise, but there were ways of apologising without saying it.

I was beginning to see much in this son-in-law of mine, not all of it was good but on the whole he was a reasonable husband for my adored daughter and for that I could forgive him a good deal.

I must have shown something of this at one time, for as Edward was walking past, he looked at me, turned, came back and said: "Madam, you look surprisingly self satisfied this day."

"Your Grace, it is the way I feel. It is a good day and I have a wonderful family."

"All at court," he grumbled and walked off. I thought, you marry a woman, you take on her family too. You knew what you were taking on, or did you not think it through in a moment of passion? Us Wydevilles are a persistent lot and are not to be shaken off. We are there whether you like it or not. And wished I could say it to his face.

I am not entirely happy about talking through this next event but the need is to be honest, there is no point in telling my story without including everything which happened and I also have a need to set the record straight on this as I have on other points. Slanders, rumours, innuendoes, you name it, anti-Wydeville partisans have managed to attach them/it to anything we have done, everything, let me tell you, from my children's marriages through distorted reports of our capture in Kent to my being involved in witchcraft. They found everything possible to throw at us, but they had no ammunition for most of it. We had to cope with rumours and innuendoes, they can often do as much damage as the truth. Outright lies, yes, we could handle them and we did. Rumours are harder to pin down, to quash and destroy.

So, Mister Thomas Cook then, and the story of the arras.

That boastful man, I can call him nothing else, acquired a very beautiful and very expensive arras which he was showing everyone who would look at it. A lot of people did, for although he was still a Lancastrian and admitted it, he had some influence and many rather powerful friends, so no one wanted to antagonise him. I saw it and fell in love with it, to the point when I wanted it so much it hurt. It was exquisite. It was a beautifully depicted hunting scene, with unicorns, nymphs, woodland creatures and many trees and plants.

He point blank refused to sell it, even though he had it in his home to sell. I would have paid anything he asked for it but he would not sell it to a Wydeville, for whatever reason. We were Lancastrian once, after all, as he was. Perhaps it was more of a personal thing; maybe he disliked his Queen so much that he decided to deny the Queen's mother that which she wanted.

Whatever the reason, I could not have that which I hankered after and so I put it to one side and said, all right, what difference does one arras make? I had lived without it up to then and would continue to do so.

Sometimes I was sure friends and helpers from the other side of the veil were on my side, other times I felt as if they were deliberately conspiring to make things go wrong, perhaps as a test of some kind, perhaps an experience I needed, I don't know. But – for whatever reason and however it was worked out, for me it all started to go horribly wrong.

Edward was being told of Lancastrian plots. Everyone knew Margaret had her spies and her informers and her cohorts busy all over England, conspiring to put Henry back on the throne. So, the plots were nothing new but the threats were getting more serious and Edward decided to make a move. He appointed Richard, my husband, to arrest those he thought were ringleaders in a plot. One of them was Thomas Cook.

Whichever way you looked at it, did that not seem as if it had been arranged so his goods could be seized and I would end up with the very arras I wanted? It was common knowledge I desired it and it looked very much, in people's minds, that was the way I would get it. At least, that is what the gossip which went round court was saying, no matter how much I denied it.

I am sorry to say I never did get it and no, the arrest was not designed to get it for me. In every part of our lives, Wydevilles had to be seen to be above suspicion because of the many who were prepared to cut our throats – physically and metaphorically – and who were just waiting for an opportunity to bring us down. They succeeded in putting a huge dent in our reputation with that particular piece of nonsense but we survived. The Wydevilles were survivors, if nothing else. And so was Thomas Cook, who came through the episode with his wealth and, it seemed, his reputation intact. He was found not guilty of the charges and was back in Edward's favour before too long. Eventually he was pardoned for his Lancastrian pursuits, too. Whilst I was displeased at being dragged into his affairs, I had no reason to be displeased with the verdict, despite comments made at the time. My ongoing displeasure was the slur on the Wydeville reputation whilst the man at the centre of it, who could have made a fortune for an arras he was anxious to sell to anyone but me, was back in favour. Sometimes I believed there was no justice in the land.

My only consolation was that there would be justice for us all when we returned behind the veil which closed us off from the other world. I held on to that knowledge as my lifeline, for I really was sore angered by the whole incident and by the aspersions being cast upon the Wydevilles yet again. All we were doing was carrying out the king's orders and living as quiet a life as we could, taking into account that we were the royal family and as such had certain obligations to carry out. Of course I knew the entire thing was based on greed, jealousy and outright enmity because of our position. I also knew that any other family who had caught the king's eye and had been fortunate enough to be associated with the crown in that way would have suffered the same slanders, but it did not help. There were even those who said the tournament had been fixed so that my son would win! Tell that to Lord Anton! He had been full of praise for Antony's prowess in the field and said so to all who would listen to him. Was it not enough that Antony had paid for the entire emprise from start to finish, to give everyone a spectacle they could enjoy and talk about for a long time? Obviously not.

Sometimes I went to my room so angry it was a physical pain in my side. It was not a good way to live. I wondered often how my daughter, seemingly so placid and calm and loving, could keep that persona in the face of the animosity shown to her at times. There were who secretly favoured Margaret of Anjou and were trying to find a way to bring her back, to displace the Yorks who occupied the central position in England. Oh I knew it, I did not tell Edward for he knew it too. He had a finger on the pulse of all that went on in London and out of it. His spy ring was vast and efficient, the Thomas Cook arrest showed that, but he was also forgiving and liked having certain people around him, so they were pardoned and welcomed and forgiven and I for one remained seething inside with anger that they should be reinstated when they had grievously offended his queen's family. Sometimes Edward could be a bit – blind? Events in 1469 showed that judgement to be true.

It was in that year that so many things began to fall apart.

Beginning with his brother's defection.

Chapter Sixteen

Word had gone around court that Clarence wanted to marry Isobel, the eldest daughter of the Earl of Warwick. Whether he had fallen for her, whether it was a way to cement his relationship with his cousin or whether it was a diplomatic move generally no one could say with certainty, or would not say, to be truthful. I asked the bowl but it remained dark, as if the problem were not for me to find answers for. It was right, Clarence's marriage or otherwise was not a Wydeville problem.

Edward made a big mistake.

Edward had a habit of making big mistakes, unfortunately. This was bigger than most: he told Clarence the answer was no. He had other plans for his brother. Now, consider this … did Edward not marry who he chose? What if our family had been as powerful, as rich, as influential as the Nevilles? He would not have had his own way in everything then, because we would surely have found a way to influence him. As it stood, all the Wydevilles had been able to do was secure good marriages and titles. It was enough for me and for Richard, but it was not enough for some families, we knew that from the talk.

I am gossiping, that will never do.

Facts.

Edward refused his brother permission to marry Warwick's daughter.

Clarence was closer to Warwick than his brother.

Warwick, Clarence, Isobel and a load of invited guests set sail for Calais and there Clarence and Isobel were married.

Direct defiance of his brother the king had begun.

Then they came back and began uprisings.

Edward began a series of visits loosely described as pilgrimages.

And I began to worry.

Clarence and Warwick were accusing Richard, John, Antony and myself, among others, of 'deceitful covetous rule.' Whatever that might mean in legal terms I do not know. It was, of course, utter nonsense and another stick with which to beat the Wydevilles. The truth was, Warwick wanted power and the best way to get it was to attack the king's family first and then the king himself.

The bowl had showed me conflict and that meant my family was likely to be dragged in yet again. That was why I worried. In truth I could not have cared less if Edward visited every sacred shrine in England provided he kept my daughter pregnant and happy and did not throw a single Wydeville out of the court or the country. He had grown larger since donning the crown, in personality and in size, not much but enough that I could see it and identify it as a trend that would continue into his old age if he did not curb his excesses of food and wine.

But his decision to visit shrines was not a sensible one at that time, I thought. My sons agreed with me and in some ways, so did Elizabeth but she had no say in her husband's activities; he did what he wanted to do regardless of whether anyone thought it was a good idea or not.

They travelled to a few places together and then things began to get a bit nasty, a few more serious uprisings upset the journeying. Elizabeth returned to London and I went there to be with her, as she was not having such an easy pregnancy at that time and wanted advice and comfort. I left the men to do 'men' things, such as round up other men and get their armour and arms ready for yet another fight. And then quite suddenly Richard and John, my fighting son, were sent to Wales to round up yet more men and Antony was sent back to Norfolk to do the same thing. My family was

163

being divided by preparations for conflict and that I did not like at all. Not a tiny bit. Travel where they will on business, yes, travel to get men together to fight, no.

Warwick and Clarence's combined army met Edward's army at a place called Edgecote on the 26th July 1469.

I have to say that on the 26th July 1469 my world began to go grey and two days later it went black.

The sun never shone again. Not in my eyes and in my mind, anyway. It was blotted out by an all-consuming hatred for Warwick.

Warwick. Immensely rich, immensely powerful but thwarted kingmaker. He thought he had Edward as his puppet king and he didn't. He thought he could direct Edward's marriage and future and he couldn't. Wydevilles got in the way. Wydevilles produced a daughter so stunning, so beautiful, so enchanting and desirable that the king of England fell for her and married her. And Warwick lost control of his one asset: the king.

And Warwick took the one thing from me that would – and did – cripple my life. He took my husband. His men captured Richard and John just outside Coventry where they had been attempting to raise a further army, held them, went through a travesty of a trial and executed them. They had no chance to say goodbye. They died far away from their loved ones, they died for the glory of an Earl who had disappointment and power combining in a heart so black even hell could not encompass it. He did not have them executed because they were the losers in the battle; he had them executed because they were Wydevilles. My only consolation was that Antony, by a miracle, had escaped his clutches, far away in Norfolk as he was, or I would have been mourning two sons and a husband.

I could not cope with the grief. It consumed me completely. I could not eat or drink and my sleep was broken by hearing him call out to me for succour, for love, for rescue.

I knew on the night of the battle that all was over for me. I was scrying that night and saw conflict, different soldiers, a different location to the ones I had seen before when I asked. I saw men fall and I saw some led away from the battlefield. When I asked if my husband and sons were safe, the bowl went black. A weight came down on my heart so hard, so fast, I thought it would stop beating altogether. I sat all night on my bed, unable to move. My ladies came and could not rouse me. My physician came, I recall his being there but he could do nothing for I could not move. I knew they were worried about me but I was devastated by the pain I felt and there was nothing I could do. Movement and speech were beyond me.

"It is as if she is in a state of shock," the physical said eventually. "I would suggest we leave her for the time being." That is precisely what I wanted them to do, go away and stop fussing over me. When I could move my limbs, when I could function again, I would be all right. Before then, leave me alone! But I screamed it in my head, not out loud.

By morning I had collapsed onto the bed and was sleeping when they came to me. They woke me and I told them I was all right, but I was worried about my husband and sons. I said nothing of the vision, I did not want to worry them or tell them what I did anyway. Worrying they understood well, they had all been through that themselves.

Forewarned is forearmed. When the messenger came with the news, there was shrieking and weeping and what I can only describe as lamentations around the Bury but I walked among it in total calm. Not peace, just calm, for I knew and I had already absorbed the

165

shock of it. There was a ray of light in the news that my golden son had escaped. But my John, my dear John, had gone. I said I thought he would not make old bones but I did not expect him to be executed. I thought he would go down on the battlefield with the blood fever burning his eyes and a fearsome grin distorting his face, as I had seen so many times when he was only practising with arms. Even then he had given his all. To think he had to endure imprisonment and certain knowledge of being executed! I was grateful, small though the gratitude was, that his father had been with him and would have encouraged him and talked him through the waiting time, the terror time, the lonely time for I knew, no matter how much talk there had been, to face death is a lonely thing. I knew it without experiencing it myself, but I had been there, I had felt it, I had sensed it from my beloved men.

I went to my room and asked for help. I had frozen inside and that would not do. I needed to function, to carry on, to demand retribution from the world for the crime which had been committed against us. I wanted to cry out the hurt so I could begin to think again.

The smell of flowers greeted me and it was with great relief I locked the door and sat down to talk with Clary.

I felt as if arms were around me, soft feminine arms and I relaxed into the embrace, letting the tears finally spill in a torrent down my face.

"Cry," she said in my ear. "Cry out the hurt. They do not hurt any more, they are safe but you are left to mourn. Cry - and then we can talk."

I did, I cried for what felt like an eternity until there were no more tears left inside me. I was empty and hurting from the effort of crying. My face and nose were blotchy and my eyes and throat ached.

"Thank you," I said eventually. It seemed inadequate but Clary knew me well.

"Now that is over we can talk, my lady. Your husband and son are beyond the veil. They are together, they are supporting one another, they are secure in the love they have for one another. They are with your young ones who did not live. You need to know too that your other son, your golden son, is safe."

I had been told this but hearing it from Clary made it something more solid to hold on to.

"Why..."

"Who can say why, my lady? Did you question why your children died? Did you question why some died at Towton, at Blore Heath, at St Albans and all the other battles yet others lived? Did you ask why when your daughter's husband was killed? Ask not now. This battle, this imprisonment, this execution, is a shame which will come back on the great Earl whether he realises it or not. He is proud right now, he thinks he rules the country but he will find his time will come. I bid you do nothing against him, let nothing come back on you. His time will come and it will not be good. It will not be a proud death. Does that help your aching heart?"

It did, in a strange way, and I told her so.

"Then ease your mind a little. Grieve for your man but hold no desire for revenge. Hate if you must, I cannot ask you not to hate, it is too big a crime for you to hold in your heart. But do not seek revenge, that will come in its own way and in its own time."

"They were not fighting him..."

"They raised men to fight against him. My lady, desist from torturing yourself. You cannot bring them back."

"I know. I have to go on somehow."

167

"I have come to warn you, my lady, that there are those who will call you a witch. Stand strong before them and deny it all. You will survive, this I promise."

"Clary, how did I manage before I knew of the life beyond the veil, before you went beyond the veil and came back to help me?"

I sensed a smile. "You would have managed, my lady, for you are stronger than many women; you are like many strong women in one body. This I admire, this I respected in you from the first time you walked in, so determined, so sure of yourself. I wanted to be like you."

"To me you were. To me you seemed independent, strong, determined to live your life your way, answering to no one. I admired you, Clary!"

"Thank you. It is a comfort to know that. You were kind to me when no one else was; you gave me warmth when no one else would. It is one reason why I come to you now, to warn you, to guide you, to help you. Your guide has told me to tell you of the accusation to come. Be prepared. Be strong. Do not let them win."

"I have too much to lose if they do, Clary. I have a family still who need my help, even from a distance."

"You are right. They need you. Others need you. Your daughter the queen will need you very much ere long, this I am told to tell you as well. Mourn for your man, my lady, but be strong for those who are left, those who will be mourning too."

Of course. In my selfishness I had not thought of them being without a father, Elizabeth, Mary, Jacquetta, all of them, my sons too, without a father and brother. I needed to speak with them or write to them, comfort them as best I could.

"Clary, thank you. You have steadied my mind and give me direction. Please thank my guide for me, too. I will be on my guard for the witchcraft accusation."

"That will be soon, my lady. Be careful. Say as little as possible."

With that last admonition the flower smell went and I was aware the room was empty of all but my sorrowing presence – or so I thought. Then I sensed a vague outline in the corner of the room, an outline of the height, size and shape of my beloved man. Before I could cry out or go to him, it had faded. At first I was even more bereft and devastated but I finally got to my feet and went over to the corner, where I walked into the most amazing cloud of love I have ever felt.

It was all I needed to make me strong. I smiled for the first time in days.

Chapter Seventeen

I had a pregnant daughter to take care of even whilst I was in the midst of total grief and despair. Elizabeth went into shock at the news of her father's and brother's execution. She was distraught and took to her bed for several days, seeing nothing, eating nothing, staring blankly at the wall, not responding to any voice or stimulus. We all feared for her sanity at that point.

Caring for her through that time kept me going, truthfully, for Elizabeth needed me more at that time than she had ever done. For one very big reason.

Edward was Warwick's prisoner.

That unbelievable piece of news flashed around the court and the country at the speed of a forest fire leaping from tree to thatched cottage to barn to tree again. It was unbelievable, people said and I heard the news open mouthed in shock – for all of a breath or two and then I saw the whole picture in one illuminated moment. I was on the verge of saying something but knew I had to think it through, carefully and slowly, without the crushing weight of sadness and responsibility on me. I put it to one side for a while, whilst I dealt with everything else as best I could but then, in the lonely hours of the early morn, I set it out in my mind and it all fitted together so well I knew it had to be right.

Now, whether I am truly right or not is a decision history will make in its own time but let me say how I saw it.

Start with the facts. Yes, here I go again.

Instead of settling the uprisings, Edward went on pilgrimages to the sacred sites around England. Then he is in Nottingham where he co-ordinates the defence of his reign and his country by sending people hither and thither to raise an army. I am not a tactician, I do not work on battlefield strategy, I see things from a woman's

170

point of view. And I see a king sending people to some distant places in which to 'raise an army'. Wales? Norfolk? How long would it take for the men to tramp their way north where Warwick's army was waiting to fight? It is almost as if Edward was making a pretence of arming himself, as if the battle to come was a foregone conclusion, as if he walked into 'imprisonment' with Warwick.

Am I being outrageous here in my thinking? This is a Soldier King, this is someone who fought his way through many battles, including the horrors of Towton, and came out victorious. Did he respect his cousin Warwick to the point when he surrendered himself to imprisonment or was this all part of a greater scheme, one which even Edward may not have fully worked out in his head but which did actually come out just as he would have wished it?

Look how it worked out.

Warwick was 'king' for a while. Clarence was heir apparent for a while. Edward was Warwick's 'prisoner' for a while and had a short rest. Then, without anyone actually saying anything out loud, Gloucester, Hastings and a large contingent of armed men arrived to escort Edward back to London - and Warwick stands back and lets him go.

Does that not all sound highly suspicious? Or is it the ramblings of a woman's mind, one who sees plots where plots did not exist, sees a pre-planned exercise where there was none, sees collusion with various people, including Gloucester – those two were as thick as thieves, everyone said – to arrange for a dramatic departure from Warwick and a triumphant journey back to London and the revival of everyone's joy at having their monarch returned to them … for Edward had become somewhat unpopular with taxes and impositions and talk of his women, his bastards and his ever growing legitimate family, not to mention his connection with the still hated Wydevilles.

I saw a calculated plan there. Maybe I saw what was not there. But, for me, it was the perfect answer to what seemed like a set of mysteries: why Edward did not put down the uprisings, why he went on pilgrimages, he who had never worried before about visiting shrines, why he allowed Warwick to take him and how easily he walked free.

Am I right? I could well be.

Will we ever know? Only if someone asks Edward outright and believes the answer they are given.

Whatever, the battle of Edgecote was a disaster by anyone's standards. My sorrow, my everlasting sorrow, is the thousands who died there for absolutely nothing and the loss, the unbelievable loss, of my husband and son for absolutely nothing, in the end not even dying whilst fighting for their king. And for that, forgiveness will be a long time coming. If it ever does.

I had to take care of Elizabeth in her grief for her father and brother and the desperate worry over her husband, for Warwick was capable of anything, as she had found out. It was a terrifying time for all of us.

Having talked of my suspicions and feelings, I need to go back a little, to just after the battle of Edgecote, to just after the – to me – disastrous, soul destroying decision to execute my husband and my son, to talk of the witchcraft 'trial.' If anything was guaranteed to strike terror into my heart, that was it.

Not long after the battle, when I was lost in grief, just as Clary had prophesied, a messenger arrived with a warrant for me to attend a court hearing in Northampton. Some nasty little individual, someone associated with Warwick, who else? had 'discovered' lead figures which he swore were created by me and were made, enchanted in some way, to cause harm. This would have been laughable had the court not long believed that somehow I had bewitched my daughter to the point when Edward had to fall for her and marry her, as he was caught under the spell I had laid on her. What utter rubbish! As if a king could not decide who he wished to marry and when! As if a man could not fall for my daughter, stunning beautiful as she was, with a glorious figure and quiet demeanour but with a spark of fire that any lover would find attractive, even if I say this myself, without sorcery! You only have to look at the evidence, how long have they been married now? How many children do they have? Yes, yes, ask how many bastards he has and I will be hard put to count them, for sure, but whose bed does he return to every night – when he can? That is, when he is not entrapped by his cousin or off fighting battles or, as happened not long after all this occurred, in exile. Sometimes there were good reasons why he was not back with her … but most of the time he was the perfect husband and returned home to his queen consort night after night. And she, being the sensible Queen Consort whom I had educated into the ways of men, welcomed him back every time, no matter where he had been or who he had been with.

Likewise the lead figures, which anyone could have made at any time, could not be proved to belong to me or been made by me.

This I say from the confident position of having survived the accusations but at the time, despite Clary's prognosis that I would come through it, I was terrified.

The messenger stood there, holding out the warrant, shaking with what looked like fear writ clear on his face. I wondered what he had been told, that I was a witch? If so, he no doubt feared I would cast a spell on him for the simple act of doing his duty. I did no such thing, of course, instead I arranged refreshments for him and sent him back to his master with – I hoped – a good impression of me and my household. As I looked at the man, before I took the warrant from his hand, I felt utterly and completely sick to my stomach, as if someone had assaulted me. The strange thing was, all the man had done was come into my presence but such was the influence of those who had concocted the charges, such was the malevolence with which they had been drawn up, that it was like a physical attack and I was hard put to stay dignified and calm whilst accepting it. I knew what it was before I opened it, having been forewarned by Clary. In that moment her reassurance that I would survive had managed to escape my mind, or had been smothered by the fear which consumed me. Inside I truly was utterly and completely terrified. The outcome of the trial, if I were found guilty, was likely to be burning at the stake. Or they could decide to throw me in prison. I could not decide which was the worst option out of that. For me to be imprisoned would have meant a death sentence anyway, I could not survive away from all that I cherished and held dear to my heart and yes, they are two different things.

Inside, truthfully, I had turned to nothing but sheer quaking terror. In fact, I went into a state of shock similar to that when I knew my beloved husband was dead but this time with tremors so bad I could hardly stand, sit or even lie still in my bed. My physician, poor man, was hard put to cope with my emotional state, eventually resorting to sedating me heavily so that I gained some relief and was able to sleep, albeit intermittently. All I could think of was 'this would not have happened if my Richard were still here. He would have defended me.' It brought it home even more what I had lost and the loss cut the heart out of me. My ladies took turns to sit beside me. They were scared stiff themselves, I knew that without them saying anything, for if I were convicted, it would reflect on them. Someone would be bound to point an accusing finger and insist they knew what had been going on. They didn't even know I went scrying, I made very sure of that. The only thing they knew was that I used to visit a wise woman and learned the art of herbal medicine from her.

But Jacquetta Wydeville is made of stronger stuff than most. Terror left very suddenly and anger took its place, anger that they should try and throw this at me, when I had just suffered the most devastating loss of my entire existence. I also saw the nonsense in it, which no one had thought through. I was supposed to have used sorcery to make two figures, one for the king, one for the queen.

Who was the queen? My own beloved daughter. Would I use sorcery, even if I had the ability to do such a thing, to damage or kill my own child? Idiotic men to even think of it. And would I use sorcery or any kind of 'magick' to damage my son in law and so damage my daughter's life and standing as a queen? Of course not. The men were even more idiotic to think I would do that.

The truth is, they had nothing to accuse me of so they went blindly into this allegation, this scandalous slanderous allegation, I have to say, with a couple of crudely made figures that could have come from any time, any hand, any place, and use it against me.

Then I thought, am I so hated? Are the Wydevilles so hated that they resorted to this kind of underhand activity? The answer had to be yes and it hurt. Everyone had pinned their hatred on one family, who had by happenstance become famous because their beautiful daughter had caught the eye of a lustful king. It could as easily have been any other family in the land. It just happened to be ours. I know I have said this before but it bears repeating, for no one seems to want to look further than what actually happened. 'Might have been' doesn't seem to have entered their woolly clouded heads. But then, they were, for the most part, mere men, were they not? Thank God I was not a man, not even the shadow of a man. I could not have endured a life of the kind they led. What led them … well, every woman knows that and how to lead them by it, too.

I had time to think all this through whilst waiting for my physician's potions and other such medicines to take effect. I could do nothing when I was shaking so hard I could not hold a cup, let alone a quill.

Once the tremors had died down, I began writing letters. I was overdue to write letters anyway, my children needed to be informed of all that had gone on. Antony needed to be contacted and told he was now 2nd Earl Rivers, whether he realised it or even liked it or not and I had to appeal to others to help me through this witchcraft fiasco. I could call it nothing less than that. Who better than those in London to whom I had been of great assistance in 1461, at the time of the uprisings? So, a long impassioned letter to the Mayor and Aldermen.

I sent up silent prayers of thanks to my guide and Clary and anyone else who had put the idea in my head, for it had come from 'nowhere' even as I was writing to Antony. It was given to me, 'why not write to those in London whom you helped?' and I thought, 'YES!' snatched another sheet and wrote the letter there and then, before going back and completing Antony's letter. I called for messengers and despatched the letters with all haste.

It worked. At about that time Edward was walking free of his 'imprisonment' and the court, which was mostly run by Warwick as 'king', fell apart and the allegations went with it. Stories were contradicted, denied, shown to be falsified and the word went out that no one held any such complaint against my lady of Bedford.

In fact, I later discovered that someone had actually lied under oath before the presiding judges. It was that close, for they were inclined to believe him.

176

That made the relief – and the fear – much stronger than it was before. It was beyond belief that someone could perjure themselves in that way just to get at me. A Wydeville. I was so grateful that it all fell apart.

But – it left a legacy which was most unpleasant. Apart from the lingering suspicions of those who believed I managed to escape from that which was a certainty, and who made sure by hints and covert glances that they still held that opinion, I still, even now, wake some nights drenched in sweat and screaming that I am innocent. My ladies come running and bring calming herbal potions for me to drink, to send me back to sleep again. The tremors come back at that time, too. It was as if the terror, it was nothing less than that, had affected my mind to the extent that it would not leave me. Clary assured me no case would ever be brought against me again and counselled me to make sure of it by appealing to Edward himself for confirmation. This I did, in January of 1470. His court heard all the evidence and stated I was completely cleared of all charges. He wrote his letter of authority confirming that, too. Even that, reassuring as it was, did not completely console and comfort me. I know why, I know full well why. It was the shock, the horrendous heartbreaking shock, of knowing I had to go through it on my own. My Richard was lying headless in some cold and lonely grave. I had faced it alone – in the living world, anyway.

I had sensed his presence several times, called out to him in the darkness when I knew he was there and took comfort from that, but – he was not physically there to support me through the terror of the proposed trial and all that it could have meant to me. I could have faced the charges with no fear in me at all had he been there. Alone, bereft of him, grief-stricken still, it was almost impossible for me to endure. I did it but I don't know how I did it.

It was a victory for the Wydevilles. If Warwick schemed that up in some way to bring the remainder of us down, he failed dismally. Then there was that dreadful Wake person, who was said to have 'found' the figures and brought the charges, there was he and some other person I vowed to track down, John Daunger. I had no doubt they were looking for a reward from Warwick for disposing of another Wydeville in a neat and conclusive way. I had no doubt there were others behind the scheme too, as it was so carefully crafted, to the point when they surely believed I could not escape their machinations. But I did.

There was another victory for the Wydevilles, too. I began proceedings against many of Warwick's men for the murder of my husband and son. I knew I had little to no chance of success but it created a storm at the time and caused Warwick a good deal of embarrassment, for he had to face the onslaught of everyone asking if he would defend his men in open court. It happened just as I hoped it would. He should not have begun to fight a Wydeville, female or otherwise, for we always, always fight back. Small victories, some might think, but to me they were enormous. It showed the world that, widow I might be, I was still a force to be reckoned with. God help me if they ever found out I actually did speak with those beyond the veil! I am right glad, and said it many times to those around me as well, that the all-seeing seer in London advised me against taking my scrying bowl to London!

My daughter's third child arrived before the Twelve Days of Christmas. She was to be Cecily, named for the Duchess of York and proved to be another sweet tempered and beautiful child. I began to wonder if the desired, longed-for heir would ever come and then remembered my going to Clary to ask that very question so far back in the past I could hardly remember the year.

As I thought about that journey, my first to meet with Clary, I heard her silver laughter, which is how I thought of it. Clary. Even her name seemed strange in my mouth at that time. I recalled my apprehension as I rode there, wondering what I would find, what sort of woman she was, would she be old, wrinkled, have a cat with her as a familiar as all such women were said to have? Did she live in a hovel, crouched over a fire, oh I thought of so many things on that ride, not least that people would call me foolish and stupid for consulting her. I was superstitiously fearful of what would happen to me when I got there and wondered again and again why I was going. I knew the truth; it was my desperation to know I would bear sons. But that did not stop me feeling apprehensive and quaking inside. That got worse the nearer we came to the cottage where the villagers said she lived.

I recalled my surprise – and no small degree of shame at my thoughts - when I arrived to find a clean, presentable young person who had no appearance of a witch, living in a shabby cottage which held the scent of flowers when none were there. The flowers which only she and I could smell and which were my lifeline and comfort in these sad tearful times. Not only these times, but countless occasions before this sadness, too.

I again wondered where I would be without her and marvelled at the ways of those beyond the veil who sought to bring us knowledge of their existence and the comfort that existence brings with it.

I thought, it seemed like a Wydeville trait, having so many girls. I produced a son after the daughters, so I hoped she would, when next she became pregnant. With Edward, triumphant, back in London and ruling everything and everyone again, I could not see that it would be very long before she was able to tell me that news. At least, I hoped it would not be long. She, and Edward, needed that son and heir desperately.

179

Chapter Eighteen

There were murmurings. There were uprisings. Provided none of my children were involved, they could all go right on murmuring and uprising. At least, that was my outward display of indifference to the goings on. Inside I was screaming, as I felt things were not going right at all.

Edward, supreme king once again, started stamping his authority on his subjects and ordered Clarence and Warwick to appear before him. They didn't. They fled to the continent with loyal followers. You can imagine how that was the talk of London at the time!

It was not good news for anyone. What does anyone do when they go into exile? They go round seeking support from anyone who will give it to them. No doubt they would end up with Margaret herself and Henry, and those who thought still he was the rightful king. Stand by for insurrection, I thought.

And I wondered how I would feel if Margaret and Henry returned, would I still be favourite, would I still be welcome at court? Following that thought was another one, did I want to be welcomed at court if she was there? I decided I did not, for it would put too great a burden on me when it all fell apart.

Now you can ask me how I knew it would all fall apart.

I went scrying and that is what I saw. First the Lancastrian arms showed themselves, with the Yorkist arms dissolving beneath them. As I looked the Lancastrian arms began to break up, to melt away like snow under sun and the Yorkist arms were once again there in all their glory.

I asked my guide if there would be conflict. He said yes. I asked if my sons would be safe. He said yes.

There, in the sanctuary of my room in the Bury, the door being bolted and barred, I cried ceaselessly. I didn't want conflict. I wanted life to go back the way it was, I wanted my husband with me. I wanted my son John back with his family. I wanted Elizabeth and Edward to create more children to see them through however long they had to live together. I wanted them to have sons to inherit the crown and throne of England. I wanted an end to all conflict and I wanted to stop feeling helpless, lonely and old.

I cried, for there was virtually none of that which could be given to me. I realised I was being hopelessly and horribly selfish and stupid, that life had to change, that there would always be conflict, men would always seek to kill one another on some pretext or other, it seemed to be their nature. Why else would they delight in a tournament where one man sought to knock out another with a battle-axe? In that moment I recalled Elizabeth putting her hands over her eyes so she could not see her husband being battered by his opponent. I wished I could do the same with my life but it had to be lived day by miserable empty lonely day.

I knew I was still a desirable catch for someone, I was still the dowager Duchess of Bedford, with money, estates and standing at court. I knew men were interested for I had heard whispers and comments but I disregarded them all. I might be lonely but I was not about to allow another man in my life and my bed. No man, no matter how wonderful or rich or handsome, could ever take the place of my Richard.

The tears stopped simply because I ran out of them. No other reason. I still wanted to cry, there was still a huge pain somewhere around my heart. My middle, my stomach, all that area hurt beyond belief. Part of it was the crying, part of it was the grief that refused to let me go.

On a sudden whim I went to my closet, took out my clothes and threw them on a chair. All of them, that is, apart from the very expensive rich black one I wore at court when in mourning for whoever and whatever. I was already wearing a black gown, one that had been made for me in a hurry after I had the news about Richard. I unbolted the door and called my ladies to me. When they came, I told them to take their choice as I was giving away all my clothes. Some, if not most of them, would have to be altered to fit their varying shapes and sizes but all were virtually new, for I rarely wore something more than two or three times, especially when at court.

They stared at the clothes and then at me. Then one asked, tentatively, what I was going to wear instead. I looked at them in turn. "Black," I said firmly. "Your next task is to get seamstresses here to make me all new clothes, cloaks, gowns, mantles, everything, in black. I will never wear colour again."

They stared at one another, not knowing what to say and I saw tears beginning to form in their eyes. "No tears!" I snapped, which stopped them from dissolving into a soggy mess and starting me off again. "I've done enough crying for the entire household this afternoon and eve. Now, help me with this. I have no colour in my life and I will have no colour in my life from now on. Take what you wish for yourselves. What you don't wish please give to others. Take them. I do not want to see these gowns and cloaks again."

They gathered everything up in their arms and hurried away, some giving me sympathetic glances that said so much, their love, their devotion and loyalty to me was amazing. They were deeply unhappy at my decision, that was obvious, but they also understood. You cannot be married to a man for as long as I had been and hold such love for him as I had and not feel as if your world has been turned inside out. There was no

182

way it would or could be turned back the right way ever again.

Father Nicholas looked at me from across the room when I gave away the clothes. He smiled and tilted his head to one side.

"You and I are now in black, my loved one." The words consoled me, for I wondered for a brief fleeting moment if I had made a mistake, whether Richard would be angry with me for giving up the colours I loved so much. Truthfully, though, I knew that it was no longer his decision what I did, but mine. In truth, as it had always been, Jacquetta Wydeville rarely took that much notice of a man, if he were on this side of the veil, anyway. There was always a way to get round a man, to guide him, coach him, make him what you wanted. And you ended up doing precisely what you wanted from the start, but you could, with skill, make him think it was all his idea.

I'm doing it again. Veering from the point, giving away too much of myself. But does it really matter?

I thought, I was accused of being a witch so I would dress in the colour of a witch. I was a widow, so I would wear black as a widow. I had a position to uphold, mother to the queen, wearing only black I would reflect back her glory, her beautiful clothes, her jewellery –

My jewellery. Should I give that away, too, I wondered.

My guide shook his head. "Enough is enough."

And it was, too. Most of that jewellery came from Richard and it would have truly broken me to give it away. I would have to consider who to will it to, though; my daughters should have it in equal shares. Elizabeth had enough already, Edward bought her the most exquisite gems but she would no doubt like some of mine. I hoped so.

That day, that night, was strange. I saw the emptiness of the closet and I endured the ministrations of the seamstress as she fussed and measured and marked and discussed and wrote down what I needed, dresses for this and for that, mantles and cloaks, muffs and hoods and all manner of things for both the summer and the cold winter to come. It mattered little that we were only in March, that the summer months stretched out before us, the woman saw a chance to make money by filling my closet again and could I blame her for that?

The emptiness of the closet echoed the emptiness of my heart and mind.

The ministrations of the seamstress echoed the fuss and bother of my ladies, determined to make me eat, drink, go out, take walks, ride, read, listen to music, do tapestries … when all I wanted to do was crawl into my bed and quietly stop breathing. Trying to live without my Richard was all but impossible.

I had to go on. I had to act the part of the aristocratic widow still living a rich and full life. Inside … inside I was falling apart. Oh, the world outside saw nothing but the woman with the determination to put her family at the top of the aristocratic tree. They saw the one who carried and birthed her babies without problems and was back at court the moment she was churched and free to associate with people again, they see the one who stood proud and tall despite being a widow and they whispered, as she passed, that she was the one who dictated policy to her daughter, the Queen, and all listened to her. Fools. They know not of what they speak. In truth, the world saw little of the real Jacquetta Wydeville. They did not know of the hours I spent with aching back and legs when unable to sit, even when carrying, because the Queen had not said we could. Margaret was very uncaring of those around her. They knew not of the smiles I put on when facing those I distrusted, most of the people in court, if I am truthful. I had more respect for those who administer the government of London than those in Edward's court. They for the most part were mere hangers-on, taking his good nature for granted. They knew not of the deep devotion between my husband and myself, I knew well they thought it a marriage of convenience for my husband, they believed he had aspired to my hand to raise himself up from a humble knight to someone with status by marrying the dowager Duchess of Bedford. They knew nothing of our love and our passion, our lasting devotion and the utter heartbreak and emptiness I suffered at his death. Those who thought him a mere humble knight knew nothing of my beloved man. Those who did not see our marriage for what it was had no marriage of their own to equal it and to see ours as a mirror of their own.

Most of all they had no idea of my burning need to ensure my family had all they needed to survive in this troublesome world, good husbands or wives, status, wealth and positions of power. They thought I did it only for the prestige of the Wydeville name. In part I did, the remainder was to ensure that my offspring were not left destitute, no matter what happened.

My Richard saw the real Jacquetta. I think at times Antony caught sight of the real person beneath the fervour with which I carried on my life. There was a knowing smile from time to time and a look as if to say 'you don't entirely fool me, Mother.' He always was the most intelligent of my brood and I admit now I was more proud of him than the other males I gave birth to. A mother is not supposed to have favourites but among that many children, it would be difficult not to have one or two I thought of more favourably than the others. I just never told them, ever.

To organise comes naturally to me. I ran the Bury as I would any other estate, with a rod of iron, to keep all in line. My children no doubt resented the discipline, the strap, the slaps, the harsh words but look at the marriages they made, look at the lives they lead, look how they have made their way in the world by being what they are, perfectly mannered, perfectly educated, perfectly suited people to the role they have in life. Put there by me. My legacy, the Wydeville children all in positions of power. They don't come much higher, when you consider positions, than Queen Consort, do they?

It was this flair for organisation that made my daughter keep me by her side as much as she could, to help with the family, the children who kept right on arriving – another was due before too long – and to advise her on how to deal with certain aspects of her life. Problems with her ladies, problems with servants that she could not quite work out how to cope with, all these came to me to be resolved. She would smile, thank me and say, "how would I manage without you, Mother?" I knew she would have to one day, I had no plans – or desire - to live forever, but before then I would do what I could to show her the best way to handle everything. But I did not dictate policy to her, that was something I left to her and Edward, as it should be.

I have to say marriage and motherhood suited her. She had a glow about her, I knew she was still a sensual woman and a very beautiful one. She was ageing slowly, her skin was good and her hair as radiant and startling as ever, without a streak of grey showing anywhere. I knew she did not colour it despite knowledge of herbs that would help if she needed it. Her hair remained its natural shade. She used a little artifice in the way of softeners and perfumes, but what woman doesn't? She was still striking enough to turn heads as she passed and it was not just because she was Queen Consort.

I have to say Antony had grown into a fine man, too. He had cultivated a small goatee beard which suited him, he wore his hair a little long, for my liking anyway, but I admit it suited him as well. He had impeccable taste when it came to his clothes, they always looked right. I knew his wife had a good deal to do with that, she suggested gently that this would be appropriate or that and he was never wrongly dressed for any occasion. I knew that he would prefer not to be in court, that he enjoyed his life on his estates or the Isle of Wight where he could relax and not be concerned about every look, word and action but he played his part, the devoted loyal brother-in-law and courtier, took part in all the jousts and anything else Edward arranged, never one to be left out. There, reliable dependable Antony, always willing, being what he needed to be in London and being what he wanted to be when away from London. Sensible, level-headed man. I was so proud of him.

I knew he was concerned about me. Not that he said anything, that was not his way. Instead he found opportunities to talk to my physician or my confessor to ensure that all was being attended to. He consulted my ladies to ask if I was eating regularly and if I slept and all the time I never, in any way, let him know I knew of his concern but I held it close to my heart and let it feed the coldness. My son cared more for me than any of my other children. Elizabeth needed me but I was useful, the others, all of them, were busy with their lives and came to see me or wrote when they wanted something. In Antony I could see much of my beloved Richard. At times that hurt beyond belief but it was good to know someone cared that much about me.

That is, the 'me' who was and is devoid of colour and of life. All that work and struggle and deviousness, which I freely admit to now, what did it gain me? Emptiness and loneliness and heartache.

But I knew no one would allow me to waste away, much as I wanted to. I had to go on. So I would, but on my terms and conditions. No colour. None at all. I would keep my jewellery but I would wear only that which was set with black stones. The more I thought on it, the more I realised what a challenge I had set myself, to present a façade to the world, the grieving widow who had retained her sense of fashion and style entirely around the colour black, but it was worth it. I had something to work at and that was valuable. Life had to have some purpose or what was the point in my still being alive?

We heard the stories.

Yes, I am about to return to the politics of the time, having diverted long enough into personal details that really I should not have revealed and yet, oddly, I feel better for having said it all. Maybe I needed to reveal it, who knows? What matters most is the world knows how totally devastated I was at the loss of my husband and my soldier son John and the bitterness I held against Warwick because of it. Oh, Clarence too, but he was a mere minion compared with the great Kingmaker who had taken lives just because he could.

In some ways, learning that they could not dock anywhere in France because no one would have them was a balm to my heart. Then we heard that Clarence's newborn son had died on board the ship that could not dock and my heart leapt with joy that they were being paid back. Warwick had lost a grandchild. Then remorse overcame me and I spent hours on my knees asking for forgiveness from Heaven and those on the other side of the veil. I should not rejoice at the death of an innocent child. The flower smell came, Clary came and still I prayed and wept and wished myself out of this life for being so callous. I only came to my senses when I found myself lying on the floor, crumpled and aching, in a swoon. I told myself I was a fool, got up, bathed my face and hands and even tried a smile. It felt strange. So strange I knew I would have to practice it in the future, if I were to live a normal life in court.

Normal? Without my husband? Impossible.

Chapter Nineteen

No one knows what went on over there on the continent apart from the people who were over there, but I could imagine Warwick not taking kindly to any of it. Big blustering man that he was, he would not have tolerated being pushed around. Edward was out of his equation; Edward had proved not to be a Warwick marionette dancing to his tune. Gloucester would go where his brother led and ignore his former mentor and cousin, for he knew well where his loyalties lie, with the Yorks. That left very little, in some people's eyes. I am relating gossip here, you understand. I had little interest in what went on, only insofar as it might rebound on my sons and how it would definitely rebound on my daughter. That narrowed my vision considerably. It had to be that way, my grief was swamping me to the point when I could hardly function some days, so I limited myself to what I knew and what I overheard and put the two together and got a sort of picture of what was going on. It was not good and Edward, apparently, knew it.

And then Warwick and Clarence returned, triumphant, recruiting men to their cause in every town and village they passed, marching through the country, generally gaining support as they went. Edward did his best to counteract it, but then he had a message that one of the major landowners in the area was about to side with Warwick and in that moment Edward decided to flee. He headed for the coast with Gloucester, Say, Hastings, my son Antony and probably half an army, knowing him. All this was conveyed to us by excited messengers, squires and others who came and went, bringing conflicting stories as they did so. Edward had turned to fight a rearguard action on the very coast of England itself, Edward had taken ship to the continent as soon as he could, Edward had left money behind, Edward had gone without money ... the stories went on and on and none of us knew for certain which was right and which was not.

My hatred for Warwick grew apace with every tale which arrived, outrageous or sensible. He had, in a moment, thrown the entire court into chaos and confusion, the king had left the country, his queen was left undefended, no one knew if they would be needed by those who were about to take over, did they have positions and livelihoods or not? It seemed almost blasphemous to think of such things at that time, but survival is everything and it is only natural that the first thing anyone thinks of is, will I still have a position and will I be paid?

Rumours flew round London like a flock of startled pigeons until we finally got the truth. What we did know, eventually, was Edward stopped long enough to send a message to his Queen and counsellors and I knew Antony sent a message to his wife for she passed on the content, well, some of it, to me. I knew that many of the men who had gone with them were left at the coast, with Antony's instruction to his wife to take care of them and then send them on their way as safely as she could, considering the mood of the country at that time.

Whether the others sent messages I honestly don't know but they didn't matter, not to me anyway. Selfish, I know, but as I said, my vision had narrowed, my life had become more restricted, my heart only encompassed that which was dear to me, my children. We knew for certain that they had taken ship and escaped Warwick's army, no doubt with every intention of gathering forces to return. There is no way any of them would abandon their country – that was an undisputed fact. The only question was, how long would it take for them to do just that?

It was good that I had organisational skills at that time. I had Elizabeth to worry about, well into her latest pregnancy, scared and without her husband – again –

and Antony going into exile with his king, out of loyalty and no doubt at Edward's command, leaving behind a devastated wife. She knew, as I did, that if your king said 'come with me!' you had no option but to go. No 'do you mind if I don't, I have a wife waiting for me in Norfolk...' that would not go down well with a soldier king like Edward. Or any king, come to that.

Like me, though, she could not bear to be without her husband. She came to London, passed on the message and then went back to Norfolk, first to Middleton, then to Sandringham and stayed there, supervising all Antony's business affairs and the estates as best she could. She had a good staff to rely on, Antony had chosen well; people she could be sure would do her bidding as if it were in his name.

My daughter arranged to gather together everything she thought she would need, with my help, and sought sanctuary in Westminster Abbey on Edward's advice. For her that was practically an instruction. In truth, it was probably the safest place because the country had suddenly become Lancastrian again, Henry VI was king once more and that made the vindictive Margaret of Anjou Queen again. And I was no longer interested in being her favourite, if in fact she wanted me to be in court at all. We had grown very far apart during the intervening years; my daughter being put in her place on the throne of England would not have gone down well. I considered, in the quiet of my room, that it was a given fact that the friendship, if ever there could have been said to be one, with Margaret of Anjou was very probably over. I was not sorry. In many ways it took a burden from me, I had enough to contend with coping with anti-Wydeville sentiments without her caustic tongue and acid mind adding to my problems.

The somewhat bemused Abbey servants and officials had no idea what to do with the queen who had arrived inside their boundaries with her three daughters, a mother and a flock of ladies. The Abbot, Thomas Millyng, hurried to find her a room, three rooms, actually. I needed one, having a responsibility as the Queen's Mother to take care of her at this critical time. I also knew she would need a midwife before too long, this child was anxious to come into the world, judging by the way it was kicking and moving, so she needed someone to supervise all that and to help her at the critical moment. Her ladies were flustered and unhappy but they knew there was no alternative, where else do you go when your court is changed very suddenly from York to Lancaster, when there is likely to be a different Queen ordering everyone around, when there is a different – if almost indifferent – king on the throne? You go into sanctuary and there you are safe, until the world returns to the status quo you had originally. I had no doubt that Edward would return, that Elizabeth would be back where she belonged, but in the meantime life was likely to be cramped, uncomfortable and very confining. In every sense of the word.

My first surprise was hearing that Margaret had not returned to England to be with her husband, who had been released from the Tower and given all due reverence by Warwick. Or so we heard. I was pleased, because as I said, I could do without Margaret's sharpness and vindictiveness, better that was left in France for the duration. I could not see this situation lasting very long. Quite why she remained in France I don't honestly know, no clear answer came to that question when I asked. She had managed to do one thing which surprised me and yet did not surprise me, she had arranged for her son Edward to marry Warwick's daughter Anne.

I knew, from talking with Antony, that was one thing which would enrage Gloucester, who had apparently coveted Anne Neville for a very long time. I knew that the marriage would not last long, though, it had been whispered to me at the very moment I heard the news. I could not tell anyone, I dared not tell anyone, the witchcraft accusations might have been dropped but they had not gone away. There were times I longed to tell people what I knew but it was more than my life was worth. I only speak of it now because now it doesn't matter. Before too long I will be on the other side of the veil and then any accusations will be immaterial, irrelevant and entirely unprovable. Am I right?

How do I know? The same way I know anything: by intuition and by knowledge that comes from those who know.

I did not know what sort of person Margaret's son had grown into, but I had every sympathy with Anne Neville having 'that woman' as her mother-in-law. There were possibly people who said the same about anyone my children were married to but one thing that could not be said about me was that I had a vindictive side to my nature.

We had enjoyed a fruitful summer of good weather and fine harvests, but the Autumn had turned cold and damp. The Abbey was not the warmest place in which to stay; Elizabeth huddled close to the fire all day, shrouded in furs, looking pale and ill as her time drew near. I fussed around her, along with her ladies, something which I confess she thrived on, arranged for a physician, Dr Serigo, to attend her daily and also arranged for her trusted midwife to be on call.

After that it was a question of ensuring sufficient meat and other foodstuffs were brought in daily to feed all of us who were living there, along with what seemed like all the Abbey attendants, clerics and servants, who shamelessly made the most of their royal visitor. I did not blame them, it was not every day that they had such largesse at their disposal. A local butcher supplied all the meat we required, I anticipate he made a healthy profit during our stay. I do not begrudge the man a single coin, he provided first class meat every single day to feed us all.

Despite Elizabeth seeming to be pale and not very well, her first son arrived with little trouble and no resulting problems early in November of that year. A fine healthy child indeed, one that would bring joy to any mother's heart. Elizabeth visibly brightened up on knowing she had given birth to the longed-for heir at long last and asked for a message to be sent to Edward as soon as possible, advising him of his son's birth. She named him Edward. We had a quick, private baptism at which the newest arrival bawled his small lungs out all the way through.

The Twelve Days of Christmas could not be celebrated as we would wish, we had to make do with some extra fine wine and candies and attending all the services that the Abbey scheduled. It was not the same and we both ached to know what Edward was doing, how Antony was enduring the separation from his wife, whether there was any chance of them returning before too long. It seemed they had been gone for half a lifetime, even though it was no more than a matter of weeks. The confining existence in the Abbey contributed to this strange sense of detachment from life, the Abbey being very old and the services timeless in themselves. The routine was rigid and ongoing, with absolutely no variations. It seemed to dull the senses.

I also realised that I had not sensed or spoken with Clary the whole time I was there, nor with my cleric either. That had to change, I needed advice and guidance. I told Elizabeth I was going to check on our rooms and make sure all was well. She agreed I should go and stretched out in front of the fire again like a well-fed cat. Her son was asleep in his cradle by her side and she was content – for the time being.

Outside the wind raged and brought ice-cold specks of rain to assault any exposed skin. I pulled my hood closer around my head, secured my cloak and with my guards, set off for the Palace and time on my own. It was much needed.

Chapter Twenty

The Palace looked much the same, apart from the fact Yorkist arms had been taken down everywhere that I could see and Lancastrian ones put up in their place. "Not for long," I said silently as I hurried past without knowing how I was so sure. I could have asked to see Henry but decided against it, there was much for the befuddled man to do in picking up the pieces of government and carrying on after Edward had reigned for a time. I thought it best to leave him to his counsellors and advisors. There would be occasion to see him, if he wished it, when all was settled. If it ever was.

The rooms were in good order, as I anticipated. I checked everything carefully and then went to my sanctuary where I sat and stared out of the window, seeing nothing but a vague cluster of very dark clouds building up, pushing the lighter coloured ones in front of them. More cold, more ice, perhaps even snow. I had best not be long in returning to the Abbey. Then I allowed myself to relax for the first time in what felt like an age. Muscles which had been tightly locked up melted into their natural softness and my body felt as if it was coming alive again. I hadn't appreciated how stiff I had been holding myself. Ever since Edward fled the country, I had been on edge, worrying, anticipating, hustling and rushing and now I had a chance to let go.

The smell of flowers surrounded me and I let myself fall into Clary's soft embrace, knowing in that moment how much I had missed her.

"My lady." The whisper came into my ear as a physical sound, not a mental one. "I have missed you."

"I too," I told her, eyes closed and ears trying to shut out the sounds of the Palace all around me.

"This time will soon pass." That was what I wanted to hear more than anything. "The Spring will come and with the Spring will come that which you desire more than anything."

"You cannot return my husband to me."

"No. What do you desire as much as that, my lady?"

"The downfall of Warwick."

"And so it will be. Wait and watch and hold fast to that which you know."

I felt a thrill go through me. The mighty Kingmaker to be brought down! Would Edward take his estates from him, shut him up in the Tower, destroy his reputation and his livelihood? What, when, how? I knew better than to ask, for I would not be told.

"Even now the king is preparing to return," she told me. This I had guessed, knowing it would not be long before Edward begged, borrowed or coerced people into helping him finance a return to his country. "And when he does, he will be restored to the throne."

"Is that his rightful place?" A question that was almost treason, but I had to ask.

She laughed and I smiled in response. It felt good. I had not smiled in an age. "In this time, my lady, who can say what is right and what is not? I would say the one with the most power is the one who has the rightful place. Think on that."

I did and she was right. If Edward swept through the country, raising Yorkist support in the way Warwick had done on behalf of Henry, then he would doubtless be the victor and then -? This time there surely could only be one king. For a moment I felt intensely sad and then thought, perhaps this is right, that monkish, pious meek Henry would be better off the other side of the veil. Someone would doubtless see to that, if only to ensure that this time Edward had no contenders for the throne.

And I wondered where that thought had come from.

January brought bitter cold winds, snow on the ground and everywhere else, it seemed, cold enough that we found ice forming on water left too far away from the heat of the fire. We simply endured, huddled round the huge fires, spending money daily on fuel, food and ale. Elizabeth moped and fussed over her son in turn. He was strong and healthy and gaining in size and weight seemingly by the hour. All we held on to was the knowledge that Edward would be doing all he could to raise men, money and ships to get back, we knew he would not and could not stay away and let Warwick reign in his place. His pride alone would not let him do that, quite apart from the fact his wife and children were here, in sanctuary, which could not go on forever. Eventually the Abbey would tire of us and the problems we created just by being there, and ask us to leave.

Hope was all we had at that time. We had messages from Edward, saying he was doing all he could. It was just enough to put life back into Elizabeth; she became interested in life again, outside of her son, that is. He had kept her going during the weeks of what we thought of as internment, unable to leave the sanctuary of the Abbey rooms, apart from the services, which were poorly attended. The country might be said as a whole to be devout but when there was snow and ice to contend with, it was a question of staying warm rather than venturing into the bitter coldness of the weather and the Abbey itself. We were fortunate, we had furs and cloaks, hoods and muffs and in extreme weather, we cut pieces of fur to slip into our boots and shoes to keep our feet warm. Rabbit fur was particularly soft and very warm. The poor of the parish had no such furs, but I am sure they too had the rabbit fur liners for their boots. Rabbits were cheap and easy to come by.

And so we struggled through January, through the celebrations of Candlemass in February and into March, with its promise of Spring and its hint of warmth. It

199

actually got warmer quite quickly, as I remember, the snow and ice leaving nothing but a bitter memory behind. We knew that with the changing of the season there was a good chance of Edward making a bid to return to England and so it was, one fine Spring day a messenger came to Elizabeth to say the king had landed in England and was making his way south by way of York, gathering men as he went.

The current gossip was, what would Clarence do? Warwick's bid to take over the country through Henry VI was obviously at risk; Edward was by far a more charismatic king than poor Henry would ever be. I am aware I consistently call him 'poor Henry' but that is how he appeared to me, stick thin, liable to fall into a state of confusion and loss at any time, happier at his prayers than at the council table with his advisors … anyone would be hard put to find a man more unsuited to kingship than he was.

Even though we hardly set foot outside the Abbey there was a palpable sense of 'something about to happen' - it filtered through to the servants and to us. We became more animated, our days passed more quickly and I began to feel more positive about the future. It was time I had some good feelings about life; it had been a long dreary lonely existence since Edgecote. I did not even have the consolation of my golden son being in the same country as me and able to visit. My granddaughters were beautiful, loving and very entertaining but they could not take the place of my husband, whom I missed hourly nor my son. I missed Antony's acerbic wit and loving manner. I hated to think how much Elizabeth was suffering during his absence. Norfolk had always seemed to me to be a very lonely distant area of the country. I also had to consider how much Antony was missing his wife. He would surely go to her before he came to me.

I was assuming he would be coming back with Edward, safe and well. I had no idea how he had been whilst abroad, he could have been taken ill for all we knew. But something told me he was alive and well. As with my beloved Richard, I would have known if anything had befallen him.

It happened very quickly after all the waiting, one moment we were sitting around the fire, the next Edward was there, striding through the Abbey to our rooms, men all around him. He was healthy, weather beaten and triumphant in every way. He caught Elizabeth up in his arms and kissed her soundly, then went to look at his son, whilst to my joy and intense pleasure, Antony came from the group of men and walked over to me. He had come back to London with Edward and was then going on to Norfolk. He hugged me and told me all was well. I could gather that from the big smile and the sense of contentment coming from him. It had been a long period of exile in many ways but I felt he had done well out of it, without his saying anything in front of Edward.

Edward was delighted with his heir and told everyone he spoke to how handsome the child was and how much pleasure it had given him to come back to such a welcoming sight as his Queen and his heir.

But he had his spies working and knew that the affair was far from over. Warwick and his aspiring forces had to be quelled once and for all. In the sanctuary of my room I saw conflict yet again in my visions and I had no doubt of the outcome, for the York arms were triumphant.

I thought on the W with the dagger through it. It could be interpreted in two ways, looking back on it. Warwick's reign ended by Edward's triumphant return and the defection of Clarence from Warwick back to his brother the king. My Wydeville heart punctured by the dagger of grief of losing my husband and son to the wish

201

and whim of the mighty Warwick. Neither had occurred to me at the time, but then they wouldn't, would they? Sometimes I wished the messages could be clearer but then, I knew well, we would not learn, we would wait for the happenings and say 'I told you so.' Life wasn't like that.

Then Edward was taking my hands. "Madam, I wish to thank you for the care and attention you have given my Queen throughout this unfortunate time. I see she has been well taken care of and my son too. I will not forget this."

Then he was off, in a flurry of orders and directions for Elizabeth's ladies and servants to pack everything up ready for his Queen to go to Baynards Castle and stay with his mother, for safety.

"I have something to do," he told her and was gone, his men with him.

Antony hugged me one last time. "I'll be back soon," he whispered. "This isn't all over yet, there are scores to be settled. But I must go and see my wife."

"Of course. She has missed you terribly."

"About as much as I have missed her!" He smiled as he settled his cloak around him again. Then he was gone too and it seemed as if a whirlwind had spun its way through the Abbey rooms and disappeared, leaving chaos in its wake, chaos that was full of happiness and hope. I turned my thoughts to all that needed to be done, so much that needed to be done!

We heard later that Clarence had ridden toward York with an army of men, supposedly on Warwick's instructions but when he got there, he went down on his knees before his brother the king and asked forgiveness. So the two groups merged and marched triumphantly on London. Warwick's reign was over. Clary was right. I was seeing his downfall and it was good, it was true balm to my heart. We also heard that poor Henry was once again interred in the Tower, out of harm's way, someone said, and Elizabeth was also moved into the Tower with her new son and her children. Lady Cecily went with her, which took a burden from me. I had been longing for my freedom in which to continue to mourn, to think, to commune with those beyond the veil. It had been a long empty time. In every respect, we had been in exile too.

Chapter Twenty One

Elizabeth told me, when I visited her in her luxurious chambers, that Edward was indeed 'back' in every sense of the word, gathering men around him, sending out arrays, clearly determined to conquer all opposition so his reign would be secure in the future. She said he was tired of constantly fighting all and sundry. It amused me much to think of Warwick being referred to as 'sundry' and I added it to my store of 'what had brought Warwick to this position' thoughts and gloated over them. Yes, I was wrong, yes, I should have forgiven but would anyone, in my position? Daily I donned black clothes as a reminder of what I was, daily I rose from an empty bed where once a loving, comforting man once lay, now lying headless in some grave somewhere that I could not visit and mourn over, not that it would have done me any good if I could or did. His absence was a constant ongoing pain that refused to leave my heart and mind. Every time I realised he was not there, my stomach turned over and a sickness rose in my throat. And that happened many times every day. I grew thin for food did not sit well in a stomach which was endlessly churning with the grief and the loss and the loneliness and I sometimes voided the food before it had a chance to be consumed. My new clothes soon hung on me and had to be altered. The seamstress tutted and fussed for the gowns were made well and they had to be taken in, which did not go well with their design. My physician prescribed and gave me physics of all kinds, some sweetened with honey which helped, some which were bitter and did not, often they made it worse. I dispensed with those as soon as I realised what was happening. I was afraid of the canker but he assured me it was not that. It was a condition of the stomach, he said, brought on by all the worries I carried. That I could believe.

I doubt anyone knew what I was going through at that time. If I had lost my husband to illness, if he had died in battle, if he had gone down on a ship crossing to or from the continent on the king's business, it would have been bad enough to live with but cold, merciless execution for doing no more than the king's bidding, no, that I could not forgive. Nor would I.

And my son, my John, to die alongside him made it unbelievably worse. I often woke in the night in a cold sweat of terror until I recalled that Antony was in Norfolk at the time and had escaped Warwick's sweep of the Wydevilles, for that is the way it seemed to me. If I had lost him too, I would not be still living. I would have found a way to end it all.

An array meant more conflict, which the bowl had revealed. A pang of fear shot through me when I realised Antony would have to go and maybe my other sons, too. A battle was inevitable, unavoidable; the forces Warwick had raised had to be crushed if there was to be peace. It seemed wrong, that there had to be war to gain peace but that was the way of it. Edward had to defeat his enemies if the reign was to continue in peace. I understood that even if I did not like it.

Elizabeth was in a torment of frantic worry and woe. She came to me with her worries, what if Edward was killed in battle, what if Warwick was supreme, what if she was no longer Queen, what if, what if … and the worry was making her ill. She too was losing weight and Edward had commented on it. We both tried to hold on to our emotions and find a calm centre but it seemed impossible. She resorted to hours of prayer; I spent time trying to communicate with my guides and helpers. I was aware Clary had not been around me for some weeks. I knew I had barriers in place and had to work to get rid of them so they, and she, could approach me.

One night, when everyone had left me, I dissolved into floods of tears, just as I had done so many times before, but this time they felt different. It was as if the tears were bitter in some way, they hurt my eyes, they hurt my throat, or at least the sobs did. I buried my face in my pillow so none could hear me and let it all go, every last part of it, all the hatred, the bitterness, the longing, the grief, all poured out in those bitter tears. When they stopped, eventually, I was gasping for breath, sore of throat and chest, my nose was running and my eyes felt as if salt had been rubbed into them. I do not wish to think what I looked like. I managed to change the pillow over for a dry one, pulled the coverlet around me and prepared to slide into an exhausted sleep.

It didn't happen.

The room became full of light, an unearthly light and I saw Clary as clear as I saw my ladies when they came to me. Her smile was radiant and I waited for, and got, her tinkling laughter.

"We have been waiting for you to do that," she told me. "We needed you to cry that hard that all is gone from you. Now we can speak."

I realised that I felt incredibly weak but empty of all those hurtful emotions which had been holding me back for so long.

"Why did it not work before? I've cried enough!"

"Because then you cried for a different reason, my lady, you cried because you were feeling sorry for yourself and because you could not take revenge on those who had hurt you so much."

"And this time was different." I knew it was, even as I said it.

"Yes. This time you cried out the hurt and the bitterness and the pain. Now you are empty and now we can fill you again."

"I cannot forgive."

"Did I mention forgiveness? We know you can't – yet - but you can stop building up the resentment and the hatred and the bitterness. This you must stop for it will damage you."

"I hurt." It sounded stupid to say it, for of course I hurt but I meant it in so many different ways.

"Yes. We know this too. The pain of losing will not go for your love was too deep but the other pains will ease. Now, sleep and we will stand guard over you."

I do not remember anything else until the morning when my ladies came, fussing over me for I was red-eyed, haggard and exhausted. But I was content inside, the fierce ache had gone, leaving only the hollowness that being a widow must surely bring if you have truly loved.

Antony was back in London, bringing my son Edward with him. They were both answering the call to arms and were full of talk, armour, weapons, battle tactics. I was upset but couldn't let them know it. There was Antony, newly back from exile, his wife and I had hardly had time to speak with him and he was on his way to battle yet again. He stopped me before I could say any of this, knowing me so well as he did.

"I have to go, Mother. How do you think it would look if I stayed behind? I would not be able to show my face in court again! And Edward needs to go, too. Do you think I want to go? I would rather be in Norfolk with Elizabeth, but - Us Wydevilles need to be there, in front of everyone. You know it's true."

I did, of course. It was simply that I didn't want either of them to go. There had been enough killing and death in our family. I did not think I could face any more.

There seemed no point in my staying in London, Elizabeth was safely in the Tower with the Duchess of York and there was, for once, nothing for me to do for her. I did not visit the Tower as there was still a bit of a prickly relationship between the Duchess and myself. Antony and Edward did not need me and the more I saw of them, the more I mourned their going into battle anyway, so I decided to return to Grafton and wait out the coming conflict and its consequences in the place I loved best. I also needed to consult my scrying bowl and I could not have that in London. My close encounter with witchcraft accusations had frightened me so much I was almost afraid to even think on it for fear of it returning to confront me again.

I also hoped that the gentler air, fresh food and cleaner water would help my stomach, which was in constant turmoil. The call to arms was not helping me very much in that regard. I wanted to distance myself from the fighting and from the fear – if I could. I know well, though, that fear travels with you wherever you go, you cannot run and hide from it. You cannot run and hide from grief, either, much as I wished I could.

I told Antony of my decision when he called to see me one afternoon. He approved, knowing of my love for our Grafton home and my need for quiet after the long troublesome winter we had been through.

I sent a message to Elizabeth telling her what I was doing, then I packed everything I needed and set out for Northamptonshire. The weather was kind, it was a mild Spring, the wild flowers were plentiful, the trees coming into leaf. As I rode, I looked at the flowers and wondered which were good for which condition, hoping Clary would be able to show me more once I was home and quietened in my mind.

We completed the journey without problems and I was back at the Bury, once more allowing its calm to overcome me and quieten me. I found my stomach settling at the mere thought of the well water, so pure and fresh, and the vegetables from our own ground, rich and full of goodness. London was a long, long way away.

There, in the quiet of my much loved home, I felt and even saw the presence of my Richard. He walked the rooms, a shadow but a substantial one. I almost reached out for him a few times but he faded away before I could even try to touch him. His smile, though, lingered in my memory and comforted me even as it brought sorrowful tears.

The news came much later, after the battle was done and the dead were counted and named and the wounded were sewn up and bound up and taken to their homes.

As far as I was concerned, the order of priorities was: Antony was badly wounded, he had been patched up and taken to Middleton where Elizabeth would nurse him back to health.

Gloucester was wounded but that did not disturb me, that man would survive anything, I did believe.

Edward, my son, came through unscathed and with commendations for his bravery.

Clarence appeared to be unscathed.

Whereas Warwick - was dead.

That last one shocked me to my core and I had to think about it for a long time before I could make sense of it.

The great Earl was no more. Some said he was fleeing the battlefield when Edward's men caught him and killed him, against Edward's orders, so it was said. Others said he died on the battlefield, fighting against overwhelming odds. Whatever the truth and only those who did the deed would know the truth, Warwick lay dead on a bier alongside Montagu and Edward's reign was secure. But at what a cost!

I was told he would be brought down, I did not believe he would be killed. I would have been content to see him a prisoner, his estates given away, his life transformed, anything but his life ending. It seemed – wrong that he should escape the retribution I wanted to heap on him for the unlawful killing of my husband and son. It seemed wrong that he should escape justice. My court case would fall by the wayside now, with no earl there to defend his men. Not that it mattered; it was to be a thorn in his side that I began it, no other reason.

My focus of hatred was gone. I had no reason to go on hating and no one to forgive. I felt oddly desolate, as if a pillar of my being had been taken away.

W with a dagger through it. How many interpretations could I have had of that one vision! But I admit freely, this was one I did not foresee. I truly felt bereft, my focus, my being had concentrated on that hatred, on my desire for vengeance, for retribution to be rained down on his powerful shoulders. And he was no longer there.

Chapter Twenty Two

Father Nicholas came to me that afternoon as I rested in my room. A gentle Spring breeze was coming through the window and taking the heat from my face. I was hot and did not know why. My stomach was quiet for the first time in an age but I felt this burning, as if my skin was on fire. I did not want to call anyone to help me, hoping that by lying down in the coolness, it would subside. I hated to make a fuss.

I wondered if it was my thoughts which were giving me the fever, as I was worrying about Antony, hoping the wound had not become infected, that he would heal quickly and be back about his business very soon. As usual, no one had sent me a message one way or the other. I had to assume if something had gone badly wrong, Elizabeth would have let me know. But then again, would she, if she was busy nursing him? Thoughts trapped in a never ending circle of worry.

To try and distract myself, I visualised the great Earl dead and the people visiting the body to convince themselves he was gone. I was also visualising the great Earl on the other side of the veil, meeting up with my Richard and John and everyone else and –

That was where the vision stopped. I did not know what he was doing. Asking forgiveness? Was he ready to do that the moment he crossed the divide? There was so much I didn't know.

I became aware that Father Nicholas was standing by the side of the bed. "Child," he said in his low musical voice.

Automatically I said; "do sit down," and we both laughed.

"You're full of questions," he said, seemingly finding a chair from nowhere and sitting down so he was on my level. "So ask."

It was odd, lying flat on my back on my bed asking spiritual questions of someone I could visualise but not touch. It was almost unreal but in reality, if I can say that, I had long since learned to accept the unreal. He was there, he was speaking with me, I took comfort from his presence and from his words.

"Where is the earl of Warwick right now?"

"Being healed of his wounds."

"Will he see my husband?"

"If he wishes it."

"Who wishes it?"

"Your husband."

"Oh." Then I understood that there really was free will on the other side of the veil. We talked for some time of what happened when you were there and how it looked from here, this side of life, until I began to grow sleepy. He stood up to leave. "I have been here long enough with you, child. It is time you rested. But do call your physician, the fever is getting worse. Before I go, let me say this: fear not for your sons, they will survive a while longer."

He left me then, with a memory of his gentle knowing smile. I put my hand to my face and realised I was burning up even more. I called for my ladies.

I cannot tell you what happened during the week that followed. I recall being so hot I could scarcely stand the coverlets on me or my night attire, I recall shivering so hard it hurt my bones and no amount of furs and covers could warm me. I was given hot possets and cold drinks in turn and nothing seemed to satisfy. I grew weak and delirious, I recall babbling nonsense and seeing people look at one another with bewilderment. I knew I was speaking nonsense and could do nothing about it. The words, if that's what they were, had to be spoken.

I knew not if anything momentous happened in the world outside my bedroom. I knew not if any family member was taken ill or wanted to see me or – it was not real. The only thing that was real was the fever and the chills and my need to sleep and eventually to stop living. It was all I wanted and it didn't happen. I fought my poor physician who was trying to pour potions down my throat, who was putting cold compresses on my head soaked in this or that concoction of herbs. I could smell them but not name them.

A night came when I was neither hot nor cold and I could hear, for the first time, Clary's gentle laugh and be aware of a cool hand on my forehead.

"Rest, my lady," she said so quietly I wondered if I was actually hearing her. "Rest and sleep. It is all over now. You have burned away the last of the grief and the bitterness and now it is done."

"Did I … give anything away in my fever?" I had to know, it was worrying me.

"Not a word."

It was enough. I slid into the first proper sleep I had enjoyed in a long time. If I dreamed, I do not remember them. I woke refreshed and ready to eat something. I tried to get out of bed and fell, I had not realised I was so weak. My ladies put me back into bed and covered me up, fussing endlessly until I sent them away to get me fresh clean cool water and fruit. I desired fruit more than anything.

They came back with water and fruit and something that did me more good than any of that, a letter from Antony.

He spoke lightly of his wound, saying it was healed and clean and he had a magnificent scar to show for his battle, then went on to say all was relatively quiet but the war was not over yet as Margaret was in the country and raising her forces for another battle. That was not something I wanted to hear, but he did go on to

213

say he was not strong enough to take part in any fighting and would remain in London. He promised to get to Grafton and see me as soon as he could.

He had not been told of my fever, I insisted no one be troubled with it, so I had a goal, I had to get strong and well before he came. He could not be allowed to see me like that, shaking, aged and in bed.

I started that moment on my path to recovery.

My hair had gone completely grey by this time. My dark hair, of which I was so proud, had begun to turn grey when I was somewhere around my fortieth year, I am not sure of the precise time but I noticed the streaks in it then and whilst I admired the grey of my husband, it made him look distinguished, I hated it in myself. The grey hairs in my brush were an affront to my eyes and my picture of myself. I think I was still visualising myself as the young ambitious girl who married Richard Wydeville out of love, lust and anything else that can be named which drives someone into someone else's arms. Ah, the times I have thought, what would I have done if poor old John had lived and I had come out of a building, whether it be a Cathedral or a mansion and seen him standing there, head of the guard of honour and if my heart had turned over and righted itself only to leave behind the total desperation to have that man no matter what… adultery is not my way, nor the way of many of the more intelligent and loyal women I knew, Lady Cecily for one. Oh I heard the stories many times, but disbelieve them all. First, there was always the possibility that the Yorks would actually achieve the throne of England and if they did, there had to be no taint attached to their reign, none whatsoever. A charge of bastardy would taint any king. Second, Lady Cecily was as devoted to her husband as I was to mine. I would not like to hear any of these stories about her repeated in the future. Heaven knows she had enough to bear

214

without that being added to her burden. I regretted often that we had not formed a friendship but the divisions between us were too great. The Wydevilles were not royal and her son had not married as well as she had hoped. I know she loved the children but accepting the friendship of the Queen's family… it just didn't happen.

I have diverted from my grey hair but that is only to be expected, as I was not happy about it. I thought of some darkening herbs but then asked myself who was going to worry? I had no man to please, not that I think my Richard would have bothered about my hair colour anyway. So, let it go. I hid it as best I could, though, under caps and nets and veils of all types, provided they were black, knowing even as I did so that the black made the grey look even more obvious. But short of wearing something like a wimple, there was little I could do about it.

So, with the weight loss and frailty that refused to leave me after my fever, I must have looked a rare sight when Antony came to see me, for he stopped dead at the doorway to my room and just stared. Then he recovered himself and came in, trying to act as if I was the same person he had left some time before.

I noticed he winced when I held him, so I knew the wound had not fully healed after all. There had to be a reason he was not going to be involved in the next battle, that was it. I looked at him carefully. There were lines in his face that had not been there before, there was a hint of weariness in the eyes, as if life had been too much for him recently and I noticed that he, like me, was thinner. Elizabeth had not been able to feed him up, but then if he was in pain from the wound, he would not have been able to eat very much. That told me a good deal, for my son was ever one for his food, often going back for more after he had eaten twice as much as anyone else at the table.

We sat for a while, making small talk, Elizabeth's health, his brothers and sisters, so after a decent interval I decided to bring it out in the open. There was no point in trying to pretend all was as it had been, after all, we had both been through too much.

"You're thinner, my beloved son."

"You're thinner, dear Mother."

We both laughed and the moment of tension between us broke and fell in pieces at our feet.

"You're tired," I said pointedly, looking at his shoulders which seemed to be bowed under some great weight.

"I am." He tried sitting up straight but the effort cost him pain, for he caught his breath and sat very still for a moment. "This is stopping me sleeping properly."

"And I had a fever which stopped me walking and eating and drinking for a while."

He smiled the rare slow smile which I remembered so well and which I loved so much. "Fine pair we are, aren't we? Good job the rest of the Wydevilles are doing well!"

"How is our Elizabeth?"

"Blooming. I don't doubt another child will be here ere long. I've lost count of how many they have between them now. Edward's fit and well and ready to fight Margaret's forces. He knows we're nearly there now, the fight is almost won."

"I wish she would write occasionally."

"She wishes she could see you, she sends her love and asks if you are coming to London soon. I'll tell her you've been ill. Maybe when you have your strength back…"

"I'll try and get to see her." I made the promise, wondering if I could keep it. London seemed a long way away from Grafton sometimes, the quiet, the peace and the solitude of the place made it an oasis in a world where battles were fought endlessly and men were killed

216

and hearts were broken. "I miss London, miss court, miss the noise and colour and intrigue but here I feel a sense of peace which I don't when I'm there. Do you understand my feelings?"

"Oh yes. It's why I escape to Norfolk as much as I possibly can without offending my king."

"Tell me about Barnet."

"What is there to tell? I led one part of the vanguard, I fought, I killed a few men, I held my position as I should - and I was not there when Warwick went down."

It was my turn to catch my breath. How did he know that was what I wanted to know?

"How were you wounded?"

He shrugged and even that hurt, I could see it. "Someone got lucky, found the gap in my armour. It's a bigger wound now than it was then, it had to be cut about a bit to get it clean."

A bit … sounded like a lot to me.

"And…"

"It's fine. No infection. Just taking a while to heal up inside, I think." He sat up and looked round. "Time's getting on, Mother, could I eat before I head back to London?"

"Why not stay tonight and go in the morning? We can spend more time together then."

He relaxed visibly and smiled again. "That's a good idea. I could do with a bit more rest. Edward can manage without this courtier for a while, I'm sure. That's if he even notices I'm not there."

That evening he spoke at length about the exile, about Hastings, whom he had disliked before they went and found it was far worse whilst they were there, of Say and Gloucester and Edward himself; "like a caged lion," he said, "ever pacing the floor working out how to get back and demolish all who had stood against him." And the moment when Clarence rode up to his brother,

217

dismounted and threw himself down in the dust, asking forgiveness. "I felt Edward's hesitation, I really did. For a moment I thought he would refuse but he was magnanimous and raised him up and embraced him. I don't think that particular relationship is going to last, though."

I wondered how he knew but didn't like to pry. It was enough for me that he was there, talking freely of our family history, how he felt when we were elevated to what was the highest position in the land. "Scared," he said ruefully. "Were we able to handle it? As it turned out, yes, we were but for a while it wasn't easy. Elizabeth found it very hard but she soon got used to the adulation." That was news to me, I really had no idea my daughter had difficulties with her new status in life. She had hidden that from me.

"And I thought I knew her well," I commented, a tiny bit jealous that Antony knew and I didn't.

"Mother, you were busy organising our lives, Father's life, all of us! How could you have known Elizabeth was uncertain about taking on the greatest and most demanding role in the country, being the king's consort? So she told me and I did my best to support her. Then, of course, I met my Elizabeth and that was another thing entirely, I had to desert my sister because of going to live in deepest darkest Norfolk! Oh I know that's how it seems to you but we're happy there."

"You're right, it is how I see it! But – oh the love you two share makes the whole thing worthwhile. So, who did Elizabeth confide in after that?"

"Jacquetta. Do you find that strange? I did until I got used to the idea."

It was strange. As children the two girls had not got on at all. Elizabeth tended to try and be superior to her siblings, especially the girls and she and Jacquetta had clashed often and violently, too. Grown up, they had obviously reached an understanding. That comforted me a good deal.

I was learning a lot about my family which I had not known. We talked of each of the children, I learned of Lionel's contentment at being in the church, of Edward's desire to go roaming, which I knew of but didn't comment on, of Richard's tendency to avoid matrimony whilst engaging in 'friendships' with any girl who caught his eye. The perpetual bachelor, that one. I had hopes of him settling down but it wasn't to be, obviously. I learned of the bitter divisions between Antony and John, which I did not know of. I told him how I had wondered that Edward was invited to Carisbrooke Castle but not the others.

"Richard wasn't interested, a castle on a small island is not for him, he prefers London. John I did not invite because I was not speaking to him – I hadn't spoken to him for many years. Lionel was too busy with church affairs. Edward I like a lot, no, more than that, I'm extremely fond of him. He's a man who knows what he wants from life and is out to get it. He acquitted himself well in the battle, fought like a demon, someone said. Simple, isn't it, when you think about it?"

"Yes, but I couldn't think about it because I didn't know about your feud with John. How did you feel when you heard he'd been executed?"

"Shocked and sorry. He had a lot of good points; he would have gone on to be a fine commander of troops. I just hope Father was able to be of comfort to him during that time of waiting. He was good in that way when we were imprisoned in Calais, so I imagine he was a great help to John."

I shuddered, for it brought it all back, the two men together waiting to die, my Richard wanting to comfort his son. It was so unfair!

I had much to think on and Antony was tiring fast, so we went to our beds. I was aware of a figure standing in the corner of my room, one that looked remarkably like my beloved husband. For the first time since I had known he was dead, I felt comforted. His presence was stronger, I could almost touch him and that helped a lot. Having Antony in the house, having been able to talk to him about things which had been troubling me for some time, to have someone to talk to about my siblings, had made all the difference to my aching heart. When my ladies left me for their own beds, something I insisted on, I reached out a hand and was sure it was taken between two strong male hands. I could have cried but didn't. Instead I felt swamped with love and fell asleep wrapped in the feeling.

Chapter Twenty Three

London called and yet Grafton held me in its charms. London meant being on show again, answering questions, coping with sympathetic looks and no doubt comments about my thinness and other things I didn't want to talk about. But London also meant my daughter, the grandchildren and being in the centre of all that was happening again.

Compare that with life in Grafton, easy, comfortable, fresh clear water, settled stomach, the ability to scry when I needed to and the privacy to cry when I needed to. Decisions! I sat quietly one afternoon and asked Clary to come to me, as I needed an answer. She came, drifting in on the cloud of perfume of the flowers, familiar and beautiful as always.

"London or Grafton, Clary?" I asked her. "London is where everything happens, policy is made, reputations enhanced or broken, whilst here-"

"Is peace." She said it with quiet emphasis. "Grafton is peace, my lady. Do you want the stomach torn up with sickness again and pain which you cannot cope with? Do you want to watch every person's eyes and hand for fear that it is set against you? I tell you this, there is a battle to come and it will not be good."

"No battle is good," I protested, half wanting her to persuade me to go, the other half wanting her to persuade me to stay. I really did not know what to do. Restless as I was, I wondered if I would be any better in London where the walls appeared to block everyone in.

"This battle will not be good for many people," she insisted. "I cannot say more, but wait for the reports. Stay in Grafton, my lady, let them fight and do what they think they have to do and do not be part of it. Then it cannot reflect on you in any way."

That seemed a strange thing for her to say. I accepted it without commenting on it. there would be time to think about it later, or more sensibly, wait and see what happened before making a judgement on the words. I knew they came from a higher authority but I could not make much sense of them.

"I am better here," I confessed after a moment. The scent of flowers stirred and flowed around me.

"Yes. Here it is pure and here you are not worried and anxious and holding yourself stiff all the time."

I had not realised I did that, but thinking on it, yes, I did, from the moment I set foot inside the walls to the time I came out again.

"I'll stay here." I said finally and with the decision made came a sense of relief so all pervasive it was overwhelming. "Thank you, Clary."

"No thanks needed, my lady. It is why I am here."

She stayed for a while longer without speaking. There was a comfort in her just being there with me.

On the 4th May Edward's army took on the might of Margaret of Anjou's force. I was told the fighting was fierce and merciless, with many dead on both sides. Among the dead was Margaret's adored son Edward, Prince of Wales.

I mourned for her, knowing how I felt when my John died. It doesn't matter how our children die, they leave a huge hole in our lives when it happens.

I also heard that Edward stormed into Tewkesbury Abbey, breaking sanctuary, dragging men out and beheading them.

I began to understand Clary's words. To break sanctuary is a heinous crime in anyone's mind. I could not believe Edward would do such a thing. I wanted to find out if it was true but the stories were mixed, conflicting and often rambling. All that anyone wanted to say was, Margaret was imprisoned in Wallingford Castle, out of harm's way, they said. It was a great Yorkist victory and the fighting was surely over.

Poor Henry, and I do it again, call him 'poor Henry' was once again put in the Tower, where he no doubt felt safe and could once again resume his pious life. I didn't know who to mourn for the most, poor Henry, deprived once again of his wife, his son and his reign, or Margaret, who had lost a son, a husband and a battle to regain possession of the throne of England.

After a lot of quiet consideration, I decided my compassion was for Henry. If Margaret had not over reached herself with her ambitions, if she had not pushed Henry to the point when he could not cope and retreated into the darkness of his mind, her son would still be alive.

In that moment I realised that Anne Neville was a widow and wondered whether Gloucester would ask for her in marriage. He had waited long enough.

The rest is soon said.

Henry 'died' toward the end of the month, whether from melancholy as some said or by assassin as others said, who will ever know?

Antony was defender of London during one last battle and Edward was secure as king of England. My daughter had no more worries. Or so I believed, anyway.

I am very tired. It has been a long recital, has it not? Forgive me if I return to my room now. For some reason my stomach pain is very bad this eve, I need to take a calming potion to quieten it. I thank you for listening, I trust you have not been consumed with ennui, that I had something to say that was of interest to you. I repeat what I said when you came, am I not royal? Of course I am and so, by right, is my daughter, the Queen of England. If nothing else, the Wydevilles have that claim to future fame.

And now, if you will forgive me …

Epilogue:

As I understand it, Jacquetta died as a result of perforated stomach ulcers. She had suffered from the ulcers for quite some time, it would have given her a lot of pain and discomfort. As the condition was not readily diagnosed, it could not have been treated. There is also the caveat that I do not believe she wanted to live any longer without her husband. Although it is a fallacy you can die of a broken heart, grief can do untold physical damage to a body.

In truth, it is as well Jacquetta died when she did, if she had seen – in this life – the decline and fall of the Wydeville family, it would have broken her completely. Her daughter's marriage to Edward IV was declared illegal, her much loved grandchildren were declared illegitimate, then consigned to the Tower and never seen again, Antony was beheaded at Pontefract Castle, along with Elizabeth's second son, Richard ... so many disasters befell the Wydevilles as, according to various reports, they fell foul of Richard of Gloucester (later Richard III). He was appointed Lord Protector under his brother's will and it is from that time that the Wydevilles lost their hold on fame and fortune. The reasons for this change with each historian's viewpoint. I can only write what is given to me.

Great dynasties often climb high and fall fast, it is the nature of the world in which we live, is what Jacquetta said about the ending of the empire she worked so hard to build. "It was good whilst it lasted," she added. "Despite everything, we left a legacy for you remember us." And we do indeed have a legacy to remember her by. Jacquetta is ancestress to all the England British monarchs from her time onward and many European monarchs, too. That is a proud legacy indeed.

Elizabeth Wydeville came to me in 2006 to ask if I would write her story and I agreed. That book is still to be written. Richard Wydeville has visited several times just to talk and in 2008, Jacquetta arrived, 'to see the person my husband visits.' If there was an element of jealousy which prompted her to make the visit, I did not detect it at the time. Apparently I was accepted, as she returned to ask if I would write of her life. It was decided her story would come first, as a book had quite recently come out featuring Elizabeth Wydeville, even if it did not meet with Jacquetta's (or Elizabeth's) approval. "Too many errors," Jacquetta told me. "Not enough research. The author should have looked a good deal further into my family."

The book was emotional to write, as her love for her husband and family was and is intense and all consuming. It was also a fascinating book to write and I am honoured to have been chosen to work on it.

You may well decide not to believe that this is a channelled book direct from spirit, that I am a good author and wrote an interesting work of fiction, in which case I hope you enjoyed your read. If you choose to believe that I channelled the work, then you will have had an insight into a period of history usually only seen through the distorted eyes of historians. There are more such insights to come from a great variety of people who have approached me with the same request, to tell their story and put the truth in front of the world.

My next book is the life of two very famous ladies, Queen Elizabeth I and Mary, Queen of Scots, the story being told from alternate viewpoints. The same criteria applies: you can take it as a work of fiction or you can accept that it is channelled from the queens themselves. Either way, I hope you will look out for it and having bought it, you will enjoy their story.

Thank you for buying this book and for reading it to the end. If nothing else, you should have a different opinion on the powerful lady known as Jacquetta of Luxemburg, which is what we set out to achieve.

Dorothy Davies,
Isle of Wight
In the year of our Lord 2010

Dorothy's grateful thanks go to:

Jacquetta Wydeville for entrusting me to write her story;
Richard Wydeville for ongoing support during the writing. He knows he is always a welcome guest;
Antony Wydeville for his constant companionship, encouragement and love. Could anyone ask for more?
Mary Holliday, devoted friend;
Ann-Jacqueline Davies, much loved friend;
Lynne Mulrooney, another dear friend who knows how much help she has been;
Terry Wakelin because he is Terry Wakelin, my rock and my anchor as always;
My Inner Circle for support, love, laughter, guidance and for always being there.

Note: at Jacquetta's request, a percentage of the royalties from this book will be donated to the Towton Battlefield Society to aid ongoing research and help finance opposition to any threats to the battlefield.